THE PHYSICIAN

First Edition

Published by The Nazca Plains Corporation
Las Vegas, Nevada
2011

ISBN: 978-1-61098-180-4
Ebook: 978-1-61098-181-1

Published by

The Nazca Plains Corporation ®
4640 Paradise Rd, Suite 141
Las Vegas NV 89109-8000

PUBLISHER'S NOTE
The Physician is a work of fiction created wholly by *Bill Smith*'s
imagination. All characters are fictional and any resemblance to
any persons living or deceased is purely by accident. No portion of
this book reflects any real person or events.

Cover, Blake Stephens
Art Director, Blake Stephens

DEDICATION

"Once you enter slavery, there is no going back. So embrace what you can learn in your new status, find the many hidden opportunities that having a stern owner can bring you, and revel in the pride your servitude can bring whoever buys you."

_____

Advice given by a father to a 18-year-old son he has just sold into slavery.

THE PHYSICIAN

First Edition

Bill Smith

CONTENTS

CHAPTER 1

THE ANNOUNCEMENT

"Glad you could come over, Chad," Adam said warmly to the athletic looking handsome man of about 30 who had now seated himself across from him. "It's been a while, buddy. Want some coffee?"

"Why not? Just black, thank you."

Adam snapped his finger, pointing to a nearby slave kneeling in the corner. It was the same strikingly handsome boy that had shown Chad in. The slave now gracefully rose from his kneeling position to fetch the coffee.

As he walked across the room, Chad was once again able to study the magnificent young slave owned by his friend: approximately 5'8", he was muscular and well defined with a narrow waist, massive chest and shoulder development, a beautifully rounded bubble butt, and had a unusually smooth creamy coffee-colored complexion highlighted by an unusual light brown hair in light ringlets framing his face, bright blue eyes, and long black eyelashes. His unusually large genitals, especially now that they were fully erect, had been banded to insure a high degree of protrusiveness, his puffy pecs were adorned with two large ringed tits, and his backside revealed the protruding ring of a well embedded butt plug, an intrusion of some depth judging by the churning of his ass muscles whenever he moved and his constant, dripping erection.

"This slave looks like he was born to be fucked," Chad commented without taking his eyes off the boy who now knelt before Chad with his head lowered as far as his thick slave collar would allow and offered the cup and saucer to Chad with both hands. "You must have a big one stuffed up him from the way he's walking," Chad laughed. "Pretty gingerly."

"Big enough to remind him of what he is and keep him open and ready for whenever he might be needed," Adam laughed. "He is a good fuck. I'm almost addicted to him, I'm afraid, to the point where it's beginning to interfere with getting things done around here."

"Ah, you'll satiate soon enough if I know you, Adam," Chad laughed. "Remember that last slave boy you had. You fucked him silly for the first two or three weeks, then you were down to about twice a day, and within six months you were so bored with him you sold him to that dealer down on Smith Road - you know, the one that specializes in fuck boys."

"You're probably right, Chad," Adam chuckled. "The boy is just one of a long line of good looking slave fresh that has warmed my bed over the past decade and hopefully, for the next decade or two," his eyes twinkled in jest.

"You've obviously got him shaved in his genital areas and in his armpits, but what about the rest of him? Was he naturally hairless?" Chad asked. "He's got about the smoothest skin I've seen on a boy his age. How old is he anyway? About 18?"

"One question at a time, and let's look him over proper. No, use him lulling around on his knees that way. Position, slave" he barked at the brown boy. The slave instantly leaped to his feet, spread his legs wide apart so his ringed genitals hung free, placed his hands in back of his head to best display his body, and tensed his muscles as he thrust his pelvis forward.

Adam reached over and rubbed the ringed nipples on the massive chest until they too were erect. "The slave just turned 19, and yes, he's body shaved but it's not needed on his chest, stomach, or butt. He's smooth as a baby in those places naturally. He's been a slave for over three years now - his parents had mortgaged him as collateral for a business investment which went sour. The bank called in the loan, so they had no choice but to turn him over to the bank, who put him up for auction. Goldsmith & Barnes, Inc., seeing a good profit ahead of them, bought him up and spent the next 18 months training him for his new life. I hear they paid a pretty good price to get him considering he was totally raw and untrained, but, of course, nothing like what they charged me for him when I bought him fully mature and fully trained. He's worked out well, though, if I don't fuck him to an early grave," his master laughed as he reached down and squeezed the slave's balls.

"May I?" Chad asked as he reached to stroke the slave's body.

"Of course, Chad," Adam laughed but continued to churn the slave's massive balls in his own hand.

Chad reached over and stroked the smooth skin of the boy's cheeks, then lowered his hand and carefully felt the massive pectoral development highlighted by the ringed tits, still erect. When Adam finally removed his hand from the slave's balls, he reached down and hefted the ball sac for himself as if weighing them in the palm of his hand and then began stroking the dripping, erect penis, watching it quiver at this new stimulation. He studied the slave's face carefully, and when the slave looked like he was about to lose control no matter how hard he tried, he ordered the slave to turn around and grab his ankles to best expose his asshole for inspection. He then grabbed the ring protruding from the butt plug and rather roughly began plunging the plug in and out of the slave's chute while the slave struggled to maintain his position and moaned deeply with each new movement of the plug.

"Hell, Chad, if you want to fuck him, you don't need to do it with that damn plug," Adam laughed. "Just pull it out and have a go at him - he's not going to object and, let me tell you, he's one damn good fuck if I do say so myself."

"Well, you ought to know, Adam. How many asses have you fucked, anyway, since we've known each other? A thousand, ten thousand, twenty thousand? Whatever, you've certainly built up an experiential base for comparisons, "Chad snickered.

"Well, this slave ranks right up there, let me tell you," Adam retorted, "and, Chad, you haven't exactly been sexually inactive during that same period. God, you've fucked my stock until they were raw, let alone all those slaves you've owned at one time or another. You're just jealous because you're poor - just two or three slaves at a time is about the extent of your bank account, it seems. My heart bleeds for you poor boys - that's why I'm always willing to share," he laughed loudly as Chad continued to pump the plug in and out of the slave's asshole for, in effect, a stand-up fuck.

"I hate to impose, Adam, but you've got me all worked up," Chad said. "Can I?"

"What else is new? Go ahead, Chad, and fuck the boy - you might as well have your dick up there instead of that plastic monster you're fucking him with anyway."

Without hesitation, Chad ordered the slave onto his hands and knees with his legs wide apart and his butt raised as much as possible. In one huge jerk, he removed the butt plug as the slave gasped from the pain of being so suddenly stretched, and then, just as quickly, rammed his own erect prick deep into the boy in a single lunge.

"Ugh! Ugh!" the slave gasped submissively as he struggled to accommodate the new invasion into his body. But he offered no resistance, no matter how much it hurt. His rigorous training had seen to that. On the contrary, he immediately began tightening his ass muscles around the invading shaft to heighten his user's pleasure.

Chad without hesitation assumed a vigorous pumping of the boy's ass and, within minutes, was gasping himself as he discharged deep into the boy's bowels in five final plunges that completely emptied his balls. Upon catching his breath, he slowly withdrew his detumescencing penis from the boy's sore ass channel, watched as the slave, fully trained, quickly turned around to use his mouth to completely clean his user's tool, and then Chad dressed as quickly as he had undressed at the invitation to use the slave. The slave again assumed a kneeling position with bowed head, but cum was now oozing from his asshole and dripping down his thighs onto the floor beneath him.

"You're right, Adam. He does fuck well," Chad announced sprightly. "Thanks for letting me use him. As usual, I owe you, buddy."

"Chad, would you put the plug back in him? Otherwise, he drips cum all over the floor." The slave immediately got on all fours and lifted his raw open hole in position for the insertion.

"Have you ever had any trouble with this slave?" Chad asked as he rammed the plug inch by inch well into the boy's rectum.

"Just once, Chad. I had him leashed to help carry stuff at the grocery store. At the checkout counter, we ran into a couple that turned out to be his parents. They'd apparently never seen their son totally naked, body shaved, his genitals ringed, and collared as a slave. They were abhorred at the sight, covered their faces, and ran for the door. Guilt, I suppose. Remember, it was they who had put the boy up for collateral for a bank loan. Well, this slave here just lost it temporarily. He started jerking on his leash, shrieking obscenities at his parents, and sobbing uncontrollably. Luckily, the store manager was there within seconds and, taking the Mylar whip he always carries for correction of the store slaves, beat him down to the floor and didn't stop until he was unconscious. The manager then gave him some smelling salts to get him back on his feet, had the store slaves quickly clean up all the blood from the beating, and we were on our way. I had this slave beaten raw every night for the next two weeks for that little episode just to make sure it never happened again. Which reminds me of something."

"What?" Chad asked.

"Slave, haven't you forgotten something?"

The slave, struggling to accommodate the reinsertion of his butt plug, looked at his owner with apprehension.

"What, master?" the slave replied meekly.

"You didn't thank my friend for his use of your body," Adam said coldly.

Fear swept across the slave's face. "Thank you, master. Thank you, master, for using my body for your pleasure," the slave quickly responded, looking at Chad pleadingly, still stuffing the plug into the slave's butt.

"Too late now, slave," Adam said. That will be 10 lashes with the Mylar whip tonight before caging so you can concentrate on being a better slave. You ask the steward to administer those to you tonight. If you forget, it will be 20 lashes; if you don't thank the steward for this correctional lesson, we'll add five more lashes."

"Yes, master, Thank you, master," the slave said with tears streaming down his cheeks just thinking about the forthcoming pain. "I won't forget to thank my user's again, Master," he added for good measure, knowing, once a punishment was ordered, it was never altered no matter what he said. He wondered if he would mercifully pass out after the fifth or six stroke of the whip, or if his body had toughened to the point where he would suffer consciously through the entire 10 strokes of the horrible instrument of pain the Mylar whip had turned out to be. It never scarred him permanently, but the pain was worse than any other whip he had ever had used on him. It was a fiendish invention that slave owners had readily adopted. He was so far into his slavery that it never occurred to him that thanking people for raping you and then thanking your owner for beating you made him even more of a slave than ever.

"Did you come over here to get your rocks off or did you have some other reason?" Adam teased. "I only ask because I can't think of a single time you have ever visited me that you didn't fuck something or other around the house."

"If you're going to be stingy, Adam, you shouldn't have let me in the door," Chad laughed. "You've got so much slave flesh around this place, you can easily spare a crumb or two for passing strangers. Besides, a good fuck always gets my mind focused on what I came to talk about to start with."

"Like what?" Adam asked.

"Like guess what I saw for sale down at Goldsmith & Barnes this morning!"

Adam shrugged, indicating he didn't have a clue.

"Doctor Leon W. Smith, M.D., Adam. I'm not kidding. Our college mate and physician. Chained up proper right on the display stands, naked and collared, all ready for auction tomorrow."

"You're kidding," Adam replied, obviously startled. "How in the hell did he end up there? I had an appointment with him no more than a year or so ago when I had that bronchial infection. At that time, he was his usual arrogant self-centered self, snapping at me as if I were an idiot. You'd think he was paying me to put up with him, not the other way around. Do they teach that smart-ass hubris in med school or did it just come natural to him? Or are those the only type of people that go to med school?"

"Wow. That's him all right. A perfect description if I do say so myself. I hadn't been to him in over a year - probably 15 months when I think about it. Anyway, the salesman told me the smart-ass bastard got a cocaine habit and borrowed so much to cover his habit, the bank finally called in his loans and before he knew it, the courts had him stripped, collared, given some quick initial basic slave training and then sold him off in a wholesale lot to Goldsmith & Barnes along with about 40 others just getting out of the state slave training facility about then. Goldsmith & Barnes has had him in extensive training for 10 months so you must have been one of his last patients before they collared the bastard. I didn't get a chance to inspect him in that the dealer was closing for the day and they were caging all the stock, but, now that his crisply starched white jacket and those fancy custom-made pure wool slacks he always wore are off him, he's got quite a body on him. Great physique, good definition, and hung like a horse. I suppose they shaped him up considerably in his training as they do most slaves, but he must have always been hung like that. He hadn't been totally body shaved yet when I saw him, so he looked strange. He's hairy as an ape generally, but they'd shaved him from his waist to his knees front and back so you see his goods up front and his bubble-butt ass. At first, I didn't recognize him, naked and all, but I thought he looked sort of familiar. Finally, it dawned on me who it was. I almost crapped on the spot. No wonder I didn't recognize him right off - who'd ever expect to see their doctor up on the block where slaves are displayed?"

"He always was a damn good looking bastard," Adam commented. "That was about his only appeal - it certainly wasn't his overbearing personality," Adam laughed. "But he's well hung, you say, and really built well now that he's had some decent training?"

"Well, beauty's in the eye of the beholder they say, but to my eye, that bastard is one sexy looking stud," Chad smirked, "smart-assed or not."

"I doubt if Goldsmith and Barnes has him up for sale if he's not properly trained," Adam counseled. "Although, I admit, it would take a lot of training to knock all that arrogance out of him. I never met a man more taken with his own self-importance. Seems to me it would take five years to get that knocked out of him once and for all. I'd be cautious in buying him, Chad; unless I was convinced he'd been completely broken to his new circumstances."

"Adam, I can't afford anything like that and you know it. I thought you might want him - you know, you could use him as a slave vet - they don't need a license - and, once you see him stripped, I imagine you could find some other uses for him - like in your bed, Adam. I tell you, he's a real looker - about as sexy as they come."

"Chad, as a vet for the slave stock, he might be OK, but most physicians don't know squat about treating slaves - they're totally ignorant of most of the common slave ailments that come about from fatigue, lots of initial stress until they adjust, and inveterate sexual usage if they're attractive. So you're better off just buying any old slave and sending him off for the six-month course in slave husbandry if you want a good slave vet. As for being a personal physician, he'd be out of date by now unless they deliberately sent him off for refresher training which I doubt, and hardly any owner would want to invest that in a slave unless he was bought to work in a hospital or clinic. There might be buyers interested in that aspect of good ol' Dr. Smith. If so, that will run his price up. But I understand slave physicians are hard to manage in hospital and clinic settings and most people have given up - the other physicians are so arrogant they won't tolerate being around slaves as colleagues - and nurses won't tolerate being bossed around by a slave. So they end up just emptying bed pans and sweeping the floor generally. So that option probably won't occur. Which leaves Dr. Smith in the same position this boy on the floor was in when he was auctioned off - just a pretty piece of slave flesh that has only his body to recommend him. Even this slave here still quietly crying about his beating tonight was a high school honor student, I understand, but that doesn't teach you much in how to be a good slave. Otherwise, this slave here wouldn't be facing a good beating tonight, now would he?" The slave under discussion choked as his crying broke into sobs.

"Well, are you interested or not?" Chad pushed.

"He might be worth a look," Adam replied. "But I'd have to be convinced he was broken once and for all to his new status in life and I don't see how that would be possible in this short a time."

"You've got to admit it would be fun to fuck the son-of-a-bitch until he was senseless," Chad laughed. "Just as an object lesson if nothing else - it would serve him right to be fucked by his former patients. Lord knows he screwed them over psychologically and financially often enough. Being owned by someone you knew would be damn humbling, I would think - especially to an arrogant bastard like him."

"An interesting proposition, Chad. Imagine if you were sold to say, me, your best friend, and made to do anything that crossed my mind. What would you do when I ordered you to bend over for a good fuck?"

"The same thing I do now, you son-of-a-bitch. Bend over and take the fuck. Of course, you usually have my mouth buried around your prick, bastard. So, in that case, I wouldn't be able to tell you just how I felt," Chad laughed, knowing Adam would understand where he was coming from since they had been off-and-on lovers for years. "I doubt if my life would be too much different, other than wearing a collar, running around stark naked all the time, and eating slave mush out of a trough on the floor if you were true to form."

"To get back to your original question, yes, I'll go and give Dr. Smith a good looking over. It might be interesting. Are you coming with me, or did you want to stay here and have another round with this slave after he's been properly disciplined tonight?" Adam announced.

"Can't I do both?" Chad teased.

"Both what?" Adam shot back.

"Look over Dr. Smith with you and fuck this slave again?" Chad responded.

"You plan to fuck the boy before or after we leave for the slave market?" Adam asked.

"Both, if it's alright with you. Visiting the market will only get me all hot and bothered again," Chad promptly stated.

"Chad," Adam laughed. "You're insatiable. The market will open at 10 A.M. Come over around 8:30. You can fuck the boy while I have a late breakfast watching you two in action, which will give us plenty of time to get to the market shortly after it opens. We can look the good doctor over thoroughly, place a hold bid on him if he checks out OK, and get back here for a late lunch and your second fuck of my property," he laughed. "It will be quite a day, especially if I decide to buy that pompous bastard you claim has been turned into prime fuck meat."

Chad jammed the last inch of the huge plug into the slave's hole with a soft groan heard over the slave's sobbing and smacked the slave's butt check in dismissal.

"Thank you, master," the young slave said meekly. He then immediately crawled to one side and assumed a kneeling position with his head bowed as he once again wriggled his hips trying to accommodate the huge plug within him.

"Have you named this property yet or do you just call it 'slave'?" Chad asked, deliberately choosing to use the impersonal 'it'.

"Yes, but I seldom use it. He's named Cofkuby. You know how I like anagrams."

"Cofkuby?" Chad looked puzzled. Suddenly, he laughed. I get it. It's an anagram for fuckboy. Perfect. Absolutely perfect."

"I like it." Adam smiled, as he reflected on his trip to the slave market tomorrow.

CHAPTER 2

THE MARKET

Adam had enjoyed his full breakfast while Chad again screwed Cofkuby, even more submissive after last night's correctional beating. The slave immediately profusely thanked his user the moment he was finished fucking him and before he began thoroughly cleaning Chad's sexual organs with his tongue and mouth.

"He did learn from the beating," Chad remarked, ruffling his hands through the slave's hair.

"There's nothing quite as instructional as a good beating with a Mylar whip," Adam said smugly. "Owners should do it more often and you wouldn't see all that surliness you sometimes witness in slaves. There's no need to put up with it in this day and age. Well, are you ready, Chad, or are you going to sit around here all day playing with my property?"

"Let's go," Chad said enthusiastically, quickly getting back into his clothes. "But remember, you said I could fuck this boy again as soon as we get back."

"Yes, yes," Adam laughed. "But I may fuck you while you're fucking the slave. You forget I may be all worked up myself by then. A threesome is always fun."

"I assumed that, you bastard," Chad laughed. "What else is new?"

Adam snapped his finger, pointing at the slaveboy. "To the slave quarters, boy, clean yourself out with three enemas, relube and reinsert your plug, then come back and thoroughly clean my quarters including washing and waxing all the floors, washing the windows inside and out, doing all my laundry including the bed linens, and scrubbing out the tub and shower. Then a complete one-hour workout on the treadmill set for 15 m.p.h. followed by 150 pushups. Then shower, body shave yourself, and, after powdering yourself, kneel by the front door until we return."

"Yes, master," Cofkuby said humbly as he gracefully left the room.

It didn't take long to get to Goldsmith & Barnes, the huge dealer just a few blocks away. The place was abuzz as it usually was when an auction was pending. Buyers were busily inspecting the wares offered prior to the sale, while slave handlers were busy sorting out the stock for order of sale, shoving the initial offerings into holding cages right next to the auction block until the slaves were so jammed they could barely move. The crack of whips was rife in the air as were the underlying hushed moans and sighs of slaves, expected prior to any big sale. All slaves knew their destiny would change the minute the word "Sold" rang out and they were handed over to a new master or mistress. Every so often, a shriek of agony could be heard as some slave was being immediately punished by an electric prod or a rawhide whip because they hadn't moved fast enough to suit their handlers, hadn't bent over fast enough to let some prospective buyer inspect their ass hole, or had flinched when some possible new owner had hefted their genitals and roughly squeezed them to see a slave's reaction to intense pain. One slave in the holding pens got overly excited and was trying to hump another slave jammed in next to him before the handler spotted it and promptly delivered a sizzling shock to the eager boy's rampant genitals, producing a particularly wrenching scream of abject pain accompanied by the handler's laughter. Another very handsome slave was pleading through the bars of the holding cage for a particular mistress to buy him - a mistress who had looked him over thoroughly, including jerking him off to full eruption to study the output and quality of his cum. A slash of the Mylar whip across the front of the slave's body by a nearby handler ended that mawkish display, although several bystanders were amused by such slavish behavior. Overall, there seemed to be at least a thousand stocks up for sale today and the place was almost frenetic in preparation.

"Where is the good doctor?" Adam asked impatiently, looking around at the hundreds of naked slaves up on blocks open for full inspection.

"Keep looking, Adam. He was clear over on the west side yesterday. He's hard to recognize without his clothes and that smart ass look on face," Chad advised.

The twosome continued to look at scores of displayed goods but to no avail. Finally, after a good 20 minutes of searching through one row after another of quivering, fully displayed livestock, Chad spotted what he was looking for.

"There's the bastard," Chad announced proudly, pointing to a slave firmly chained to his stand with a tall thick collar around his neck, his genitals fully banded for prominent display, and rings welded through both extended tits. The slave held his head as low as his collar would allow and tears were streaming down his cheeks as one young teenager, barely 14 or so, was playfully stroking his fully erect shaft and roughly massaging his ball sac while another, even younger, was playing with his ringed tits. The fathers of the two boys busied themselves checking out the slave's musculature and ass.

As Adam and Chad approached the display stand, they overheard the conversation taking place.

"He'd make a good bedbuck for Thomas, don't you think, Glenn. Tom seems attracted to him already and every 15-year-old needs something around to keep them off the streets and properly amused."

"Well, Bobby sure likes to play with his tits, it seems. If you don't buy him for Thomas, I may pick him up for Bobby. He's not old enough to fully appreciate what the slave could offer him, but he'll grow into it. In the interim, the slave could warm my bed now and then," the other father winked. "He's got a nice ass, don't you think," the man said as he quickly slipped a finger up the slave's ass hole and wiggled it around, emitting yet another moan from the slave on display.

The other father waited patiently and when that finger was withdrawn, he inserted his own and pumped the slave's ass with it vigorously. "He probably is a good fuck," the other father announced. "I see what you mean about using him now and then yourself - not a bad idea. Although I hardly want you to end up bidding against me. Might you be interested in buying the slave jointly? That way both our sons as well as both of us could enjoy him around the clock. He looks sturdy enough to hold up to those demands."

"Great idea. That way we can bid higher and probably get him. Thomas and Bobby," he said to the two still eagerly playing with the slave's prick and tits, "guess what? Your dad, Thomas, and I are going to bid for the slave together as a present to both of you. But if we get him, you'll have to promise to share him with us."

"But daddy," Thomas whined, "I wanted a slave all for my very own."

"And so did I," Bobby pouted. "I want a slave that belongs just to me so I can have him around all the time. I don't want to share him with other people fucking him and sucking him off and all. It would just ruin it for me."

"These brats are really spoiled," Thomas' father announced dejectedly. "It's their mother's fault, giving them everything they want the minute they open their mouths. But I'm not going to fight city hall, are you, Glenn? If they want their own slave, I'll go along with it, but nothing priced this high. No way. Come on, Thomas, we'll find a slave all your own we can afford, not this luxury item."

"But I wanted this buck, Daddy," Thomas whined again, accompanied by his 14-year-old friend.

"Shut up or I won't buy you any slave today. I don't want to hear any more whining or it's home we go, empty handed, and you'll be back to jerking yourself off every night," his father said sternly.

The two boys did shut up, took their hands off the slave they were playing with, and promptly followed their father into the section offering older, used, and generally less attractive slaves that would be considerably cheaper.

"Kids nowadays," Bobby's father commented exasperatedly to Glenn as they led their sons to the cheaper section for the purchase, this time around, of two bed bucks. "You just can't please them."

With that group gone, Adam and Chad were free to fully examine their former physician. When Dr. Smith looked down at his new tormenters, he instantly recognized his two former patients and blushed bright red from the top of his head clear down to his toes, his humiliation was so complete. His tearing turned to riverlets and he broke out into an anguished sob until a handler heard it and promptly smacked him across his back with a rawhide whip.

"Quiet, slave, while you're being handled by your betters," the handler said as he lashed the slave once again for emphasis. "You know better than this," he warned as he again raised the whip and watched the slave give him a frantic look of raw fear.

"Yes, master," the doctor said promptly to avoid the lash coming down again.

"My apologies, sirs," the handler said pleasantly. "Just a little correction. I certainly don't want to discourage you in looking this property over thoroughly any way you want. It's just that this slave has taken us a long train to get properly trained and we sure as hell don't want to see all that training go for naught. He's broken now, but it sure took a lot of doing," he laughed as he reached over and pinched one of the slave's tits who grimaced at the pain but never flinched. If we could break this bastard, anyone can be broken to slavery," he announced rather proudly. "He was one tough cookie, let me tell you."

"I can imagine," Adam said as he reached out and hefted the slave's swollen genitals and began to churn them in his hand. "He used to be my doctor - not a bad doctor, maybe - but a real arrogant son-of-a-bitch completely sold on himself. Slavery is probably the best thing that's ever happened to him."

The slave under examination again broke out sobbing in shame and humiliation as his former patient played with his balls and shaft. Again, the rawhide whip quickly slashed across his back, causing another round of unbearable pain. He screamed in agony as the lashing had come with full force across the already aching areas of his previous lashings.

"I don't know," the handler said disgustedly, "whether this bastard is totally broken or not. I've heard there are a few that never break and you just have to sell them for body parts and write off your loss." He raised his arm again, took aim, and really came down on the slave's back and shoulders this time around in a series of blows which finally knocked the slave down to his shackled feet, blubbering in his intolerable pain. Raising the whip threateningly again, he ordered the slave to his feet to display himself properly for inspection.

The slave struggled back to his feet (which was difficult with his hands shackled in back of him), spread his feet wide apart so his banded genitals once again hung freely, and thrust his pelvis forward as he gasped for air. His body was wet from the perspiration of raw fear and stress.

"What do you say, slaveboy?" the handler asked him coldly.

"Thank you, master," the physician said humbly between gasps with pure fear in his eyes. "Thank you."

"There. That's better. Now let's start over with this inspection. He's all yours, gentlemen," he said with a little flourish of his hands as he folded the whip back in readiness.

Adam lost no time checking out the slave's tackle, stroking it to full erection, while Chad stuck first one finger, then two, then three up the slave's hole checking out his fucking capabilities. Both twisted and tweaked the slave's ringed tits until they too were full erect and raw. Before they were through, the two had gone over every square inch of the slave's body and probed every bodily orifice to their satisfaction. It was an examination a medical doctor, always in a hurry, couldn't even fathom. As a final touch, they stroked the slave until he had a full ejaculation right in public up on the stand and then proceeded to taste the cum, commenting to the audience they had attracted in their examination that the slave's cum production was not only prodigious, but tasty - even sweet - having none of the sour taste you often find in caged animals. The slave himself looked totally defeated and his face reflected whole new levels of utter shame at being publically humiliated in this fashion by two of his former patients and college mates. At last, the hollow look of a slave's total subservience and utter obedience replaced any trace of his former arrogance and pomposity.

"What do you think, Chad?" Adam asked as he wiped his fingers off in the slave's hair. "Shall I buy him? He might be good to fuck and I could certainly use him as a chauffeur and gardener. I sold the last one I had just last week. One of my friends was smitten with him after I let him fuck the slave, and bought him right on the spot - for a very hefty profit, I might add. This slave here just might fill the bill. I assume he can drive - after all, he certainly had his fill of BMWs and Mercedes in his day - the gardening, under a heavy whip of course, would keep that body in good shape and well-tanned, and I assume his basic slave training has included taking a good fuck as well as offering up his body for any other pleasure an owner might seek with it."

"Buy the bastard, Adam. I'd like to whip the shit out of him for being so damned arrogant to me back in college. Maybe a good fucking would ease my feelings a bit, but I'd still like the pleasure of just beating him for no other reason than that I can."

"Good reasoning, Chad. That's exactly what I planned to do. A daily beating just because he's my property now and it will be good for him. And, yes, I do plan to fuck the shit out of him to teach him a little humility. Oh, don't worry, Chad, I'll give you a go at him too."

The slave under discussion looked horrified and turned white in raw fear. No one paid any attention as the time of the auction was approaching. He was unchained from the stand, whipped to a nearby holding pen, and pushed in against the writhing bodies jammed inside. His time for a new owner was upon him.

Adam and Chad patiently waited through 14 sales before Dr. Leon Smith was chained to the auction block. Among the comfortably seated bidders were three main competitors for the pending sale: an administrator at a local medical clinic, an owner of a nearby metropolitan football team, and a middle-aged businesswoman running an upscale escort service. Adam chatted amiably with them despite their competition over the slave being auctioned. The clinic administrator was interested in the slave's medical training and his reputation as a physician. The football team owner wanted the slave as a team physician who could also serve as an easily accessible sexual outlet for his high strung team of athletics. He elaborated on this latter use by pointing out a lot of the time the players on his team wanted their sexual needs met almost immediately, and fucking the team physician was as good a use of the slave as anything else, especially since he was quite appealing in the looks department. The businesswoman wanted the slave because of his educational level, his upper-middle class background, and a body that would look very appealing both in and out of clothes. She explained her rent-a-slave escort service provided either female or male slaves to singles wanting a companion to the opera, the theater, a major league ball game, or a cocktail party who had considerable poise, good manners, and charm but were also good in bed before the evening was over. Slaves in her service had to be well behaved, versatile, and sexually open to any and everything their renter might come up with. She had examined the doctor several days ago and was satisfied he could fill the bill, especially since she kept her stock very disciplined and the slightest customer disappointment led to severe beatings. She did share the information that the slave was fast "recycling," which meant, she explained, he could be easily brought to orgasm five or six times in a row with proper stimulation.

The slave being auctioned, Dr. Smith knew exactly what was happening, of course, and anxiously awaited the outcome, knowing he had no control whatsoever of what was happening to him. He silently prayed that no one who knew him in his previous life would buy him, preferring sale to either the clinic where all the other staff would despise him and assign him work others wouldn't do, the football team as their sex toy where he knew he'd roughly be fucked near to death by the brutish athletes, or the escort service where at least he would get some sexual contact with women even though he was reduced to a whore. Any of these were better than an even more humiliating sale to his former patients.

First, the clinic manager dropped out of the bidding, saying it was too much to pay for a bed pan cleaner, because that was usually where slave physicians ended up due to their lack of acceptance by free doctors and nurses who refused to take orders, even suggestions, from slaves. He could buy a janitor for a lot less than that. Next, the team owner backed out, pointing out it was hard to get team members to accept treatment from a slave, physician or not, and he could easily pick up a good looking hunk for the team to fuck at their leisure at half the cost this slave was going for. Finally, the escort agency owner dropped out, stating the price was getting too high to make much money on her investment. Slaves in her escort service were usually worn out or looked haggard after about three or four years, so you had to get them cheap enough to make them pay for themselves in that short a time. There was spirited bidding up to this point, but Adam persevered, edging out each bidder one by one until the property on the block was his.

When "Sold" was shouted out and the slave looked up to see Adam and Chad smiling, he knew his fate was sealed. He had no control, of course, but he knew his days as a slave would get worse, even worse than the horrors of the severe slave training he had undergone over the past many months. He gulped and turned ashen as reality hit home and a leash was attached to his slave collar for delivery to his new owner.

"We'll just walk the slave to his new home," Adam explained to the sales manager of Goldsmith & Barnes as he approved the sales price to his charge card and took delivery of the sales certificates. The manager thanked him for his business, and promptly handed both the leash and the standard slave whip to Adam. "Don't be afraid to use it, sir," he urged when he handed the whip to Adam. "This slave has been in training for 12 long months and shouldn't cause a bit of trouble, but it's going to take a firm hand to keep him that way. I'd strongly recommend a through beating - at least 20 lashes - each and every day - to remind him of his status now. And, of course, absolute control of all food and water as well as all bodily functions to remind him constantly he's totally under control of his owner from now on: you should make every drop of water, each morsel of food, each emptying of his bladder, each getting his rocks off, each minute of sleep - be under your absolute control and privileges which he has to earn by pleasing you in every way possible. Finally, I'd fuck him regularly. Nothing like taking it up the ass to remind you, you're a slave. Do all that, keep him on sparse rations so he's always a little hungry and thirsty, and work him as hard as you fuck him. With that, you shouldn't have a bit of trouble. Don't do that, sir, and you're going to see, day by day, a slow return of what he once was and you'll lose every bit of your investment in a damn good looking slave, if I do say so myself." He reached over and fondled the slave's genitals as an affirmation of his last comment. "Oh, one other suggestion, sir. I'd definitely keep this heavy tall collar on him and that genital band and those big tit rings. They all serve a purpose, you know."

"Thanks for the suggestions," Adam said sincerely. "I plan to do all that and more. You see, I knew this slave some time ago before he was enslaved. He was an arrogant, cocky son-of-a-bitch that really doesn't deserve getting off just being enslaved. But I'll make sure we keep this bastard from ever getting close to what he once was, or at least thought he was," Adam said as he calmly removed the leash from the neck collar and rebuckled it to the slave's genital ring. "He'll mind better this way," he smiled as he jerked on the leash and the slave audibly moaned as his balls were stretched before he could catch up with his new owner who briskly walked with his friend back to his house. As he trotted along behind his former patient, he focused as best he could on each step so that the leash didn't tug on his genitals more than they already were. People snickered as they saw the naked slave's plight in trying to keep in coordination with his owner's tight leash and laughed at his prominent erection. Even more amusing were the tears streaming out of the slave's eyes and his deep blush of humiliation at this new public degradation. The slave recognized several of his former patients enjoying the scene and it was obvious in their faces - they were quite glad he had come to this turn of events. "Served him right - arrogant bastard" was written all over their faces. There wasn't a hint of concern or compassion present in any face he encountered. Little did the physician know what was ahead of him.

CHAPTER 3

COFKUBY AND THE NEW SLAVE

"You want to be the first to fuck him?" Adam asked Chad as they walked along the street, the new slave in tow by his balls behind them.

"You bought him, Adam. Surely you should have first honors," Chad replied.

"First honors, my eye. Dr. Smith has been fucked 1000 times at least in Goldsmith & Barnes' training program and you know it. Have you ever known of a slave going through training that wasn't fucked at least three or four times a day? That's probably the most effective part of their training. Now, I repeat my question, would you like to be the first to fuck this slave's well fucked chute in my era of ownership?" Adam asked.

"Tell you what, I'll fuck that Cofkuby boy I had this morning again while you fuck this slave. Then, we'll switch," Chad suggested.

"You're on, Chad. I knew you'd come up with some practical suggestion when it comes to enjoying ourselves with the slaves."

By that time, they were going up the front steps of Adam's townhouse and, sure enough, Cofkuby was, exactly as ordered, kneeling by the entryway with his head bowed, his body freshly cleansed inside and out, shaved, and powdered.

"Get your ass into the sitting room, Cofkuby," Adam commanded. "My friend wants to fuck you again."

"Yes, master," Cofkuby answered as he swiftly moved to the adjoining room and, getting down on all fours, spread his legs wide and lifted his ass for the impending use of his body. As he did so, he was able to glance at the handsome new slave being led into the room by a leash attached to his genital ring. Although the slave was considerably older - probably in his late 20s - he was in top shape, beautifully proportioned, very muscular, heavy hung, and almost delicate in his handsome very manly facial features. Cofkuby felt his prick swell as he studied his master's new possession.

"You, Dr. Smith," Adam commanded in an icy tone, "get down in the same position as my other slave. "Your new owner, your former patient, wants to fuck you."

"Yes, master," the slave blushed as his genital leash was jerked once again, pulling him close to his new owner so that the leash could be unfastened from his ring. As soon as it was removed, he quickly got down on all fours like this younger slave and spread his legs wide apart, remembering to lift his ass up as he'd been trained over and over.

Without hesitation, Adam had shred his clothes and plunged his rampant staff all the way up his former physician, who moaned submissively as the shaft penetrated deeper and deeper within him. The slave grimaced from the pain, but never moved from his commanded position, struggling to adjust to the very large organ driving into him unrelentingly. When the shaft was all the way in, Adam began vigorously pounding in and out of the slave, enjoying the slave's attempts to stifle his screams of pain and anguish at this latest raping of his ass hole.

Chad followed with Cofkuby, but at a more relaxed, less frenzied pace. The young boy was a delight to fuck and Chad appreciated his baby smooth skin, his pumping of his user's embedded shaft with his well-trained ass muscles, and the acceptance, even pleasure, the slave seemed to be receiving in his fucking. Chad noticed the slave's own prick was hard and dripping throughout the fucking, a clear sign the boy had learned to enjoy being screwed - at least on the physical level. He looked over at Adam's brand new slave, Dr. Smith. The new slave's prick was fully hard and dripping also now that his body had adjusted to the initial pain of the assault on his ass. Apparently, Goldsmith & Barnes had done a good job in preparing the doctor for his new role in life, including training him to enjoy what was inevitable in the life of any good looking slave - again at the physical level. As he continued pumping in and out of Cofkuby, he wondered if the good doctor was enjoying his fucking at a more cognitive level as well. Time would tell, he thought.

"You like getting fucked?" Adam asked Cofkuby as he was vigorously being fucked by his friend. It was one of the few questions he had ever asked the slaveboy.

"Yes, master," the slave dutifully answered. Adam reached over and smacked his ass while continuing to pound into the doctor's exposed hole.

"No, Cofkuby. I mean do you really enjoy it - not do you accept your master's rights to your body?" he asked again.

Cofkuby looked confused. When did a master ever ask a slave whether they liked anything of not? He answered cautiously. "I like whatever pleases my master," he said. His owner's friend continued to pump unabatedly into his hole during his owner's interrogation.

Adam again reached over, delivered another smack on Cofkuby's ass, then reached under him, and gave a strong pull on one of Cofkuby's tit rings. Cofkuby knew he had again given a wrong answer as the pain from the tug on his tits raced through his body.

"I repeat, Cofkuby, do you like getting fucked and I better get a straight answer this time or I'll tell the steward to give you 25 more strokes with the Mylar whip tonight for your impertinence."

Cofkuby turned white in fear at the threat, issued so casually without a moment's pause in his master's friend fucking him.

"I do now, master, but I hated it for a long time," Cofkuby answered.

"Elaborate, slave," Adam ordered.

"Well, master, at first I hated being raped worse than any other aspect of being a slave. But, when I realized I wouldn't have any other form of sex as a slave, it at least made me feel sexual and a few times you let me shoot off, master, when I was being fucked. So now, master, I admit, I like it - it's better than nothing, master."

"Well said, slave. One more question. If you were a master and had a slave, would you fuck him regularly?"

"Of course, master. Aren't all slaves fucked by their masters?" Cofkuby answered, sort of confused. "A master would be stupid not to fuck his slaves whenever and wherever he wanted."

"Yes, all slaves worth looking at are certainly fucked regularly by their masters. And, yes, it's certainly a master's right and privilege to do so."

That said, Adam increased pounding into Dr. Smith's asshole until he felt the familiar result of such action. He plunged in as far as he could go and released a huge stream of hot cum into his new slave's bowels, just as a similar event was happening in the pair next to him.

When Adam had withdrawn from Dr. Smith's hole, he said, "Cofkuby, plug yourself immediately so you don't drip all over the floor, then fix Master Chad and I a refreshing cold beer."

"Yes, master," Cofkuby replied as he quickly got to all fours, grabbed his plug and, squatting to best open his hole, gently reinserted the plug trying not to grimace in the process until he felt it snap into place fully embedded, and then headed for the bar to fix the drinks. He was thirsty himself, but knew better than to mention it, let alone take a drink himself.

"And you, Dr. Smith," Adam looked at his new slave, "stand up and face me real close. I see you enjoy being fucked from the looks of that huge hard-on you're sporting and I want to stroke it a bit while I chew on those big juicy tits of yours. I want to discuss your future duties with you other than just getting fucked. We've got a litter of nice young boys around here just for that - you've got to earn your keep over and above that," he laughed.

"Yes, master," the slave meekly replied, gritting his teeth in dread.

Adam grabbed the slave, pulled his right tit up to his mouth, and began vigorously sucking and then chewing on the swollen ringed nub. When it was fully erect and sensitive, he did the same to the slave's other tit, all the while stroking the slave's erect and dripping shaft. But, after a few minutes, he ceased his tit play and concentrated on roughly massaging the slave's ball sac as he spoke.

"First off, you're my new chauffeur, which means you will drive me wherever I want, help me in and out of the car, and wait patiently for me in the car when I'm on an appointment, errand, visiting, or shopping. You're keep the car spotless at all times, both inside and out, or you'll feel it on your hide. Next, you'll be my gardener - there's only the back garden in this townhouse, but you will keep the grass clipped daily, the flowers watered and weeded, put in new plantings as needed, and keep everything neat and tidy. You will workout on my exercise machine for three hours daily when you're not doing something else - we want to keep your physique in top shape. You'll be strapped to the machine which is programmed to shock you appropriately any time you're not putting forth maximum effort. By the time the machine is through with you, you should be so exhausted you can barely walk, but you'll recover soon enough. Any failure to work with the machine the full three hours daily will lead to a beating you won't soon forget. Every night, even if you've done everything absolutely to perfection, you will still receive 10 lashes with the Mylar whip from the steward just for being my slave; 20 more lashes if you've disappointed your owner in any way whatsoever; and 5 more if the steward feels you're not putting forth your best efforts at all times. Of course, we will add to that for specific misdeeds as necessary. You can only have food and water as specified by the steward at the appointed times - usually twice a day. You can only piss and shit when ordered to do so - any unscheduled will be severely punished. You can never touch your genitals or tits in any way unless specifically ordered to do so; you can never ejaculate unless you are ordered to do so. You will body shave completely every day except for the head on your hair and a small pencil-line beard I plan to have you wear around the edge of your jaws along with a pencil-line mustache I think would look good on you. You're so damn hairy I want every drop of hair off of you - armpits, ass crack, chest, everywhere. You will oil your entire body after every shaving and you will douche yourself after every fucking at the first available opportunity. Of course, the steward will clean you out completely every morning with several enemas as soon as you have had your morning dump, so you'll always be fresh and ready if somebody wants to fuck you. In your remaining time, I'm going to send you out to the plantation farms to check all the stock out medically and identify those that need to be sold off, treated if they're worth it, or disposed of. You should be able to check at least 50 or so thoroughly every day in the three of four hours you'll be there. We've got 10,000 slaves out there currently, so that will take a while. Any slip-ups in that area, doctor, and you'll be sent back to the training school for the special disciplinary program they reserve for rogue slaves of one type or another. If that happens, you'll be sold off after that - you'll be so damaged after that program I won't be interested in your body anymore."

Dr. Smith shuddered, but it was hard to tell whether it was from the rough handling leaving his balls extremely sore or his dread of what his future held.

"Adam, how are you going to dress him up as your chauffeur?" Chad asked.

"Simply, very simply, Chad. He's wearing his uniform now," Adam responded.

"You mean he'll be out in public, standing by your car at full attention, as bareassed as he is right now with only his collar, tit rings, and genital bands to cover him?" Chad laughed. "Perfect, Adam. Perfect. Especially since so many of his old college chums and former patients will get to see him like that - they all go to the same places you go to so everyone will get a good look, if not the chance to personally inspect him." Chad chortled at the image. "You going to let them fuck him if they want?"

"Probably. A good public fucking is always instructional for a slave, Chad, especially one from a background of unmitigated arrogance and hubris," Adam replied. "It helps them focus on the reality of their current status."

Cofkuby delivered the cold beers and then knelt at his master's feet. As the two men enjoyed their beers, Adam ordered the doctor to get on his back. As soon as he finished his drink, he wanted his friend Chad to fuck his new slave where he could study his face as he was being fucked. When Chad was ready, he ordered the doctor to place his legs up over his shoulders to best expose his hole and, putting his drink down, proceeded to climb onto the slave, jam his tool deep into the slave's open hole, and started pumping as the slave shamefully stared into his eyes - a look that reflected his utter despair at being so humiliated and knowing there was nothing he could do to prevent it. Adam, inspired at this new position, ordered Cofkuby on his back for a similar face-to-face fuck, which the slave readily complied with. These couplings were longer than the first and it was a good 30 minutes before both of the men had emptied themselves into the slaves' holes, now raw and bruised from the constant pounding. Both slaves were crying from the pain, but the doctor's tears weren't just from the pain - they were primarily tears of utter despair and total humiliation. Now, as never before, he truly felt like a slave - a mere property at the disposal of his owner. It was one more step into a world from which he would never return, even if he were miraculously freed one way or another, and deep down in his soul he knew he was a slave for life, regardless of what happened to him.

That night, the doctor was administered the 10 lashes he had been promised for just being a slave and 10 more because he forget to thank his new master for fucking him. The pain was unbearable but he knew he would have to get used to it - there were no options. The steward administering the beatings told him this was for his own good and the Mylar whip was especially instructional in the making of a good slave. Perhaps he was right - it certainly taught you the complete control and power a master had over you and simply obliterated any thoughts of rebellion, backtalk, or refusal to obey any command whatsoever. He desperately needed to piss and shit, but knew he couldn't until morning when he would be allowed to do so. Likewise, his ever rampant prick screamed for orgasmic relief but he knew that too was forbidden a slave. Even getting a drink of water would have to wait until the master allowed it. The fact he could accept these things told him he was sinking deeper and deeper into his slavery. Strangely, it didn't frighten him. Somehow, he knew that at some point of total acceptance, he would find a modicum of happiness in his slavery - a happiness that only came with total acceptance.

Cofkuby, apparently the master's personal servant and main fuckboy, was caged next to him. He reached through the bars and gently grasped the doctor's still erect penis. "Maybe the master will let me fuck you for his amusement," Cofkuby said gently. "If so, I'm certainly looking forward to it. But, if it's the other way around, I want you to know I'll certainly enjoy being fucked by a good looking slave like you - you turned me on the minute you walked in the master's door."

"Good for you, whoreboy, but get your hands off the merchandise. You know we're not allowed to get off without permission. What are you trying to do? Get me beaten even more, faggot?"

"Oh, whoreboy and faggot is it, asshole? You let them fuck you just as I did without a hint of resistance. Besides, I saw that big erection when they were fucking you. You liked it just as much as I did. I bet you like it with men better than women and you're old enough to have known both. Me, I've never had to chance to be with a woman so I don't know if I'm a faggot of not," Cofkuby said, releasing the swollen shaft under discussion. "Not that it makes much difference when you're a slave anyway if you think about it."

"You're right, slave. I'm sorry I called you those names. You didn't deserve it any more than I do," the doctor said. "If you are ordered to fuck me tomorrow, enjoy it for all its worth and I'll do the same - it's all we can do," he sighed. "I certainly won't hold it against you. Besides," he glanced over through the bars into the next cell, "you're a mighty fine looking piece of slaveflesh yourself. No wonder they bought you to fuck - who wouldn't, given the chance?"

"I heard them say you had been a free doctor before you were enslaved. When you were free, did you own slaves?" Cofkuby asked.

"No, I was always too busy to manage them properly. I didn't even have a dog or cat because I didn't have time to feed them and I was seldom home. My only contact with slaves were the janitors at the clinic who I never spoke to, of course, other than issue some orders now and then, and some whores I rented pretty regularly to drain me when I felt horny. Until I was placed in training, I didn't have a clue as to what life was like for a slave or even much what was expected of them."

"I'm sure your training changed that fast enough," Cofkuby chuckled. "I was enslaved long before I had much exposure to slaves, male or female. So everything I know I've had to learn since I was collared. My parents had mortgaged me for some of their crazy business ventures. When the mortgage was called in, I didn't have a clue what was happening, but here I am, being fucked over and over and picking up after the master, keeping his quarters clean and spotless in between flushing out my insides and lubing for the next round. I never dreamed this is what slaves did - I was so naive when I was sold - although I admit I would do the same if I was a master. Well, we better get some sleep. No telling what our owner has in mind for us tomorrow." With that he rolled over in his cramped cage and fell promptly asleep. The doctor did the same, the bruises from his beating turning from raw pain to throbbing ache, his prick still dripping in need.

CHAPTER 4

THE SHOPPING TRIP

The next morning I was delivered to my new owner filled with a small ration of slave chow and a quart of water, completely scrubbed inside and out after my morning piss and shit, body shaved to his specifications, and well lubed. He promptly ordered me to lean over the side of a divan with my legs spread wide and proceeded to thoroughly, let leisurely, fuck me until he was completely drained. All the while, Cofkuby busily went about fixing his master's breakfast, his ass cheeks straining to contain the huge butt plug inserted by the steward after his morning hygiene. As soon as the breakfast was prepared, Cofkuby presented it to his master's table just as Master Adam finished fucking his new slave.

"Cofkuby, I'm got a treat in store for you today," his owner said cheerfully as the new slave finished cleaning his owner's tool, sticky with cum and lube. "I'm going to let you fuck my new slave here and - if this breakfast is as good as it smells - I'm even going to let you cum while you're doing it. It's been a while since I've let you shoot and your balls are getting awfully tight. Shooting off in the new slave's ass will fix that, I fancy," he laughed.

"Thank you, master. Oh, thank you, thank you," Cofkuby said excitedly. It had been three weeks since he had last been given permission to shoot off and his balls felt like they were going to explode from the pressure. "Thank you, master," he said once again, truly grateful for this opportunity to alleviate his chronic need.

"Doctor, get down on all fours, so Cofkuby can fuck you now doggie-style," Adam ordered. "It will be fun to watch you getting fucked again while I eat my breakfast."

"Yes, master," the doctor answered, wondering what it would be like being fucked by someone practically young enough to be your son, although, thinking of the 15-year-old he might have been sold to as a bed buck, this would certainly be better than that. Cofkuby was very heavily hung, however - much more so than his new owner or his friend Master Chad who had fucked him yesterday. Never mind, he thought. He certainly wasn't bigger than the training dildos jammed up him in his training, let alone the slave studs that had fucked him over and over after he'd been properly stretched with the dildos in the later stages of his training. Being fucked by another slave on command, however, was never as humiliating as being fucked by your owner or his friends. Slaves had to do what they were told. The masters did it because they could, knowing the slave could do nothing to prevent it. So even though it was humiliating to be fucked by a mere kid, the kid was still a slave and had no choice in the matter. Somehow, that made it considerably less humiliating. Besides, Cofkuby had told him last night he was hoping he would get to fuck him - and his wish had come true, even if it was only for the master's breakfast amusement.

Cofkuby lost no time in his assigned task, promptly mounted the older man, inserting his large shaft up the slave's lubricated chute, and began vigorously pumping as his hands grabbed the slave's shoulders for balance. He knew better than to cum right away or it would spoil his master's entertainment. Therefore, he exercised every control to sustain his pending eruption until he saw his owner was getting bored with the show and was about to finish his breakfast. At that point, he let go, began fucking with total abandon until the slave beneath him started scooting forward with each thrust and, with a throaty animal roar, shot over and over and over into the older slave's rectum. Cum was leaking out of the slave's hole in profusion as his ass quickly filled and was already all over the floor beneath them. He glanced down and saw the older slave, this former doctor, was struggling to keep from shooting off himself, begging "Master, Master, can I shoot?" between his gasps.

"Oh, very well," he heard his master say.

With that permission, Dr. Smith's body shook in orgasm and in heave after heave, he shot all over the floor until a huge pool of steaming cum was beneath him while both slaves were still bucking and heaving in one intertwined bundle of sweating flesh.

"Thank you, master, thank you," both slaves said simultaneously. "Thank you," they uttered once more and it was obvious from their utterly sincere tone both were truly grateful for this rare opportunity to drain themselves. At that moment, both slaves truly loved their master for his kindness and concern. Such moments were yet another step into their own slavery, but they could care less. The relief from the chronic need of weeks and weeks was overwhelming and their master cared for them or it wouldn't have been allowed. It was a privilege rarely allowed a slave by any master and they were unfeignedly grateful.

"You, doctor, lick that mess up off the floor, and, you, Cofkuby, get a wet rag and clean both of you up. Then, doctor, as soon as you've douched all that cum out of you, we're going shopping today, and you, Cofkuby will clean the house and do the gardening while we're gone. The doctor won't have time for the gardening today if he's to get in his three hours of rigorous exercise."

"Yes, master," both slaves said at once. Cofkuby ran to get the cloth while the doctor dutifully started licking up all his own hot cum as well as some of Cofkuby's that had already run out of his asshole. He could tell which was his and which was Cofkuby's by the temperature: his was still warm; Cofkuby's had cooled down already as it had dribbled out of his ass, but both had a nice fresh taste although Cofkuby's, he noted, was a little milder, typical of teen-age slaves, he'd learned at the training school.

After Cofkuby had cleaned him off externally, the doctor went into the adjacent bathroom and douched himself as ordered. He noted the bathroom, like those in the slave quarters, was fully equipped for just such tasks. He then reported back to his owner, kneeling at his feet.

"All ready, doctor?" his master asked. "We'll be taking the BMW 7 Series today," handing the slave the keys. "It's in the garage along with the others. Pull the car out to the front, and then wait for me kneeling by the opened back door. I won't leash you until we go shopping."

"Yes master," the doctor responded, quickly taking the keys and leaving to find the garage. Within minutes, he had the maroon car in place and was kneeling by the opened door.

Quickly his owner emerged commanding his slave, "We're going to the Southhampton Mall this morning, doctor. Park as close to Brooks Brothers as you can."

"Yes, master," the slave answered as he gently closed the door and rushed around to the driver's position, again carefully closing the door so as to not disturb his master. He was bothered that he was out in public totally exposed, but realized there was nothing he could do about it if that was what his new owner wanted. At least, right now, he wasn't showing hard, although his banded genitals were still very protrusive and eye-catching, especially now that he was fully body shaved.

The mall wasn't crowded that morning so he was able to park the luxury car close to the Brooks Brothers store as directed. He immediately ran around the car to open the door for his master, oblivious to the stares of some teen-age kids skateboarding out on the parking lot who started making some very lewd and suggestive comments about his complete nudity, his ringed tits, his banded genitals, and his tall slave collar. He blocked their comments out as he knelt by the opened door until his owner emerged, leash in hand. The doctor dreaded being leashed by his genitals in public as had happened yesterday, but knew there was nothing he could do to alter the situation. When he felt the click of the leash on one of his tit rings, he felt nothing but gratitude toward his master, especially since the teen-age boys were watching, who, he knew, would have much preferred to see him leashed by his genitals. Nevertheless, being leashed in this fashion was no picnic - the slightest misstep led to terrific pain as the tit got stretched or twisted.

"Slaves behave better when you leash them by the balls," one of the more brassy teen-agers advised his owner. "Be happy to do it for you, with all due respect."

"I'm sure you would," Adam answered cooly. "When you buy your own slave, you can leash him any damn way you want. Until then, I'll leash him my way, thank you."

The teenagers made some insulting remarks under their breath and then sped away on their skateboards, the fun being gone from the event.

Adam jerked on the leash, watched as the slave's tit stretched in the process, and briskly began walking toward the store. No sooner had he entered, then an officious clerk suggested he leash his slave to the "convenient retaining rings by the front door, especially, sir, since it isn't clothed."

"I'll keep the slave with me, if you don't object more than you already have, and, as far as I'm concerned, the slave is clothed. Can't you see he's banded?" Adam said in an icy tone that put the clerk in his place. "Now, please show me to your slacks. I'm looking for some of light wool, tightly woven, and tobacco brown or slate gray. Maybe one of each if they fit properly."

"Yes, sir," the clerk said, apparently properly put in his place. He glanced down at my banded genitals, once again erect with a drop of pre-cum on the end of my cleanly circumcised shaft, with obvious envy and lust in his eyes. He quickly found what Adam was looking for and, when my master was trying them on in the fitting room, he took the opportunity to feel my pec development, play with my tits, and even hefted and churned my balls. I knew my master would object if he knew what was going on, but he didn't, and it was certainly a slave's lot of endure such incidents without objection when they occurred, which was rather frequent when a slave was out in public, especially when you were displayed stark nude.

As the clerk continued his ball play, he studied my face. "Say, aren't you Dr. Smith?" he asked. I nodded. "You're the guy who treated me for gonorrhea, remember? About two years ago - I had it bad - picked it up at a whorehouse you thought from one of their slaves. Well, I'm surprised to see you a slave now, but that's what happens sometimes. You just never know what's ahead of us," he philosophized as he began stroking my shaft. "You still doctoring?"

I nodded no.

"Oh, I see," he said, quickly releasing me when he saw my owner returning.

"I'll thank you to keep your hands off my slave without permission," Adam said icily to the clerk.

"Ah, I just bumped into the clumsy bastard," the clerk replied.

"He's not clumsy and you've been playing with him - look, he's totally erect and dripping like a stud horse, thanks to you. I should report you to the manager. Slaves are at the disposal of their masters, of course, but you're sure as hell not his master."

"I'm sorry, sir. It won't happen again. I shouldn't have touched your property, I know. Please don't report me to the manager. I'm about to lose my job as it is. I'm really sorry - I just got carried away - he's so damn good looking and all." Tears welled in the clerk's eyes. "Please don't tell the manager. Perhaps you'll like a pair of those slacks free of charge, sir, to make up for my indiscretion. That way you'd just have to pay for one pair if you decide to take both."

"Very well, I won't report you this time, but I will take you up on the free pair of slacks. It's the least the store can do to make up for this breech of decorum. It's hardly the slave's fault."

As Adam paid for one pair of the very expensive slacks and got the other free, he handed the package to his slave to tote. Before leaving, he advised the clerk. "Keep your hands off of other people's property, no matter how attractive they might be. In the interim, save up your money and buy a cheap slave for yourself - no matter how old, worn out and ugly. You can at least play with them all you want - you can fuck them to death - and no one will give a damn. But other people's property - hands off! You can pick up some dredge down in the holding pens for less than a month's salary nowadays with the glut of slaves on the market."

The clerk looked at my owner with total respect and thanked him profusely for the advice. "I never dreamed I could own a slave of my own that cheaply," he exclaimed. "Of course, I'd have to pay for some slave chow now and then, but still, no matter what they looked like, I could still get my rocks off regularly."

"Exactly. Maybe then, young man, you could keep your hands off of stock like this," he said as he again jerked on my tit leash and we were on our way into the interior of the mall. The interior was considerably more crowded and there were few slaves heeling behind their masters who weren't clothed in some fashion or another, although some might as well not have bothered their outfits were so revealing. But I was the only one I saw that was totally nude and certainly the only one banded on full display so I drew considerable attention. Many commented on my good build, my handsome looks, the size of my equipment, or my ringed tits which were quite protrusive themselves, having swollen over the months since they're were ringed to about thrice their original size. The tit leash also drew considerable comment. My owner enjoyed the attention I was drawing and especially enjoyed my embarrassment at being publically displayed in this totally humiliating fashion.

"Blush all you want, boy," he said, again jerking on my tit leash. "This is what slavery is all about as far as you're concerned. And you might as well get used to it; because I plan to display you just like this every chance I get. Besides, it's a good lesson for a slave once so arrogant and cocky. This sort of thing is what will help keep you in line if anything will. You're just lucky you have a damn fine looking body - at least you don't have to be ashamed of that in any way. Imagine how you'll feel if you weren't hung like you are. If we get a chance, I'm going to see about getting you fucked in front of a crowd. That will teach you humility like nothing else."

Tears were streaming down my cheeks as I noticed the leering stares, heard the ribald comments about my body and the use it was no doubt being put to every night, and all the suggestions to improve this or that about my decorations and adornments. My master was right. It was the ultimate humiliation and I truly felt like a total slave, just an owned piece of property being displayed for my master's amusement.

"Look at that slave's prick," one cheap-looking teen-age girl said loudly to another. "How'd you like to have that thing drilling you every night?"

"I would if I could afford it," the other trashy girl replied, licking her lips suggestively. "And I bet he licks pussy well, too."

Two eight-year-olds stopped and starred at the slave's ringed tits, apparently not having seen such devices before. "Why are there rings in that slave's chest pimples, momma?" one asked. The other chimed in, "And, momma, why is that ring there around that slave's great big popo?"

"Oh, it's just a slave, boys. Sometimes people put those things on them, but really, he shouldn't be out here naked in front of respectable women and children," she said, taking the boy's hands and leading them away from the sight.

"Momma, when we get a slave, can we decorate him like that?" the doctor heard one of the children asking the mother as they left while the other chimed in "Why aren't all the slaves naked like that - I think it looks good and besides, it's a lot easier to tell who's a slave that way."

"Well, those are good points, Johnnie, but let's get on home now. Mommie has lots to do."

A huge unshaven man, rippling with muscles himself, and dressed like a cowboy, took one look and then approached my master. "What to sell that dude? I'd pay plenty for a stud like that."

"Just bought him myself. Ask me again in a year or so and maybe we can strike a deal," my master said cheerfully.

"Will do, chap, will do. But only if he ain't fucked out by then."

"Just out of curiosity, mister, what would you do with this slave if I did sell him to you?" my master asked. "That is, if you don't mind my asking."

"Hell, I don't mind. I'll tell you - I run a stud farm a few miles out of town. He's just the type I'm looking for. I've got 18 to 20 good studs on hand, but I can always use another one. You never know when those boys are going to play out on you - especially studding at the rate I keep them at. They're only lasting four or five years before they run completely dry or their sperm ain't worth spit. Constantly on the lookout for promising new ones. This boy here shows a lot of promise if he's not just all show and has got a lot of little pups hidden down in those big balls of his." He laughed and, with a nod from

Adam, reached over and churned my balls through his rough hands. "Feels good and there's lots of juice in this boy. If you ever want to sell him, here's my card," he said reaching in his shirt pocket.

"Might do that if the price were right," Adam said courteously. "He'd probably make a good stud like you say. It would certainly be a switch for him. Right now he's mainly on the receiving end." Adam turned the card over and began to read it.

"Don't doubt that. You'd be a fool not to poke something like this every chance you get."

Adam studied the card: "Williams Stud Farm - Satisfaction guaranteed or your stud fee refunded. Prime studs ready for your inspection and use. Why buy when you can breed them for a fraction of the cost and get exactly what you're looking for?"

"You busy out at the farm?" Adam asked as the man continued his complete examination of the doctor's genitals right in front of everyone.

"Right busy. We've got so many owners of female stock bringing them out to be fertilized the studs I've got on hand are humping round the clock. Can't keep them at that rate much longer or they'll dry up on me no matter how much I whip'um. That's why I've got to get some more studs out there this week. I especially need some big black studs. People are demanding them more and more, it seems. I guess it's a new fashion, but suddenly everyone wants blacks and I've only got one black stud in the barns. He's about tuckered out," he laughed, but I'll probably locate at least two or three more at the auctions coming up tomorrow. Still, I could use a boy like this, even though he's not black. He's still mighty attractive and his git would probably reflect it, no matter what old cow we mated him with. Everyone wants studs that are hung heavy, it seems, although you and I both know that doesn't have a damn thing to do with fertilization rates. I suppose they want the offspring heavy hung if they're male. They know they're getting more when they market them that way."

"Interesting business," Adam said, "but I've got to be going. "I'd like to visit your operation someday if you allow visitors."

"Come on out," the cowboy said. "It's fun to watch the boys in action, and we can have a beer together while I offer you a price for this boy you can't turn down." He released his hold on the doctor's genitals and wiped his hands off in the slave's hair since the slave was wet with pre-cum by this time. "Mighty fine slaveboy," he said as he strolled away.

The slave was left standing fully erect with the package of slacks still in his arms.

"Come on, doctor. I've got to pick up a new battery for my videocam." Adam jerked on his tit leash and they headed for the electronics shop a block or so away, with the doctor dripping pre-cum along the way. Fortunately, the store had the correct battery and the sale was quick, but not before the manager asked if he could inspect the "beautiful slave you own."

Adam granted permission, but said he was in a hurry. The manager grabbed the doctor's ball sac, weighed them in his hand, and then proceeded to stroke the erect prick until some more pre-cum oozed out of the tip.

"Better let up or the slave's going to make a mess," Adam advised with a quick jerk on my leash. I instantly groaned from the pain coursing through my body from the stretched tit. "Good doing business with you," he said to the manager as we made a quick exit back to the inner mall.

CHAPTER 5

THE LADY IN THE BAR

"I need something to drink," my master said as he glided me into a swank bar. Once my master was seated on a barstool, I knelt at his feet with my head lowered. Adam ordered a beer for himself, but never inquired (or even thought about) whether I was thirsty or not. I was dying from thirst by this time, but knew better than say anything.

As my master was sipping his cold beer, I noticed another slave kneeling nearby, leashed by his collar. The slave was not a day over 20, exceedingly handsome and beautifully built with muscles rippling everywhere. His waist was exceptionally small for such a well-built man which made his chest and rump even more pronounced. Outside of his thick collar and his large 2" tit rings, the only article of clothing on his shaved body was a pair of extra-low-rise Jockey briefs about three sizes too small which clearly revealed every detail of his balls and prick as well as his bubble-butted ass. His owner had left intact his full head of thick, curly blonde hair, a pencil-line well-trimmed beard outlining his jaw, and even his light covering of body hair except, from what I could see through the tightly stretched Jockeys, all the hair around his genitals and ass which had been shaved smooth. His eyes were particularly striking: large, dark blue, with long thick lashes and jet black brows. He couldn't hide his huge erection about to burst out of the tiny Jockey briefs.

His owner, apparently a middle-aged woman of no beauty, was talking to another older unattractive woman at the bar. Within minutes, there was a jerk on his neck leash and he was ordered to his feet.

"He's great in bed, Phyllis," the one holding the leash said. "He's so well trained by now he can fuck for hours and never shoot. Besides, that," she said reaching over to the slave and cupping his genitals through the stretched material of his briefs, "he's well-equipped for his duties as you can see for yourself. He's a good licker too if you like that."

The slave under discussion blushed in embarrassment and shame, but, as a slave, he knew better than to do anything that could possibly be construed as resistance of any type. But the slave kneeling nearby me saw his look of utter defeat and complete humiliation at being owned as a mere sexual plaything by a rich lady. To her, he was a sexual toy, not a person, and both slaves in that bar understood that completely.

"How much was he, Alice?" Phyllis asked.

"Too much! But I guess it's worth it. Four hundred and thirty five thousand to be exact. But I'll get a lot of that back when I decide to sell him. Boys trained this well only depreciate 5 to 10% a year on the average. So, it's a luxury, but well worth it! Besides, he's so young and eager."

Phyllis moved over to the standing slave and ran her hand slowly across both his butt cheeks, squeezing them gently, before moving to his chest and tweaking his large hanging tit rings until the slave's tits were swollen and fully erect.

"Here', Phyllis, feel for yourself," Alice said as she took Phyllis' hand and moved it to the slave's crotch. "He's always ready to go, Phyllis, and he's hung just like you like your slave meat - long and thick - super-sized."

"He's perfect," Phyllis agreed as she squeezed the slave's genitals. "Hung like a damn horse, a body like Adonis, a face that's gorgeous, and skin like a soap ad. How much just to use him?"

"For you, sugar, nothing at all. Bartender, you got a couch or a room in the back where my friend here could use my slaveboy?" Alice asked.

"Of course, madam. There's a cot in the back with a pile of fresh sheets nearby. Just have your slaveboy remake the bed with fresh linen when you're through with him."

"There you go, Phyllis. Fresh linen and everything. All you need is some good solid slaveflesh and here it is!" Alice said triumphantly as she handed Phyllis the slave's leash. "Have fun - and let me know what you think of him."

Turning to the slave, she warned, "you perform well, slave, or you'll wish you had the minute I get you home. My friend here deserves the best and that's exactly what you're going to give her, you hear?"

"Yes, mistress," the slave said obediently, again blushing deeply as he saw another slave staring at him as he was led to the back room by his neck leash, his owner's friend already gripping his genitals through the skin tight briefs and massaging him to a full erection.

A look of total resignation clouded his handsome features.

Adam was as fascinated with the handsome slave as the woman taking him lustfully to the back room to service her. He stuck up a conversation with the owner of the fine-looking slave.

"I heard what you paid for that slaveboy," Adam said. "That's a lot of money."

"Yes, but worth it - at least so far," his owner, Alice, replied pleasantly, her eye's sweeping across the slave at Adam's feet. "Your slave is no slouch in the looks department either and he's hung as well as my slave it looks like. Is your slaveboy well trained?"

"He's new to slavery, but, so far, he's working out fairly well. Time will tell, I suppose. I don't know quite how to put this, but is your slaveboy fully trained to please all types of potential owners?" Adam queried.

"You mean servicing men?" Alice laughed. "Of course. I've frequently loaned the boy out to some of my male friends for their pleasure."

"Glad to hear it, madam. I'll cut to the quick. Would you be interested in having this slaveboy here at my feet service you while I bedded down your slave? The trade could be fun, don't you think?"

"You're on, Mister. Just as soon as my slave is through pleasuring Phyllis." She laughed. "From the sounds of it, it won't be too much longer. Sounds like he's doing a good job. Phyllis has always been a screamer when she's with a good stud."

I blanched when I realized I had just been "loaned" as a stud to this strange lady my owner had met in a bar and that I would have to satisfy her in every way she wanted or face a beating that night I wasn't sure I could survive. As soon as the deal had been made, the lady ordered me to my feet and began hefting my balls, stroking my shaft to a full erection, and massaging my swollen ringed tits while I blushed in shame and tears silently slid down my cheeks in my embarrassment.

"I take it you're protected," Adam warned. "This slave tested out fully fertile."

"Oh, don't worry. That slave of mine tested out the same way, but a woman who owns male slaves always protects herself one way or another. Some of my friends have had their male properties' balls removed as a convenience, but me - I'm still on the pill. It's a lot easier than paying for all those castration fees."

Within minutes her friend Phyllis emerged from the back room flushed and with a sheen of sex sweat on her followed by the borrowed stud. He was soaked with sweat with his beautiful curly hair matted to his head and with every muscle still in full contraction. His prick, still fully erect and throbbing, was more than evident through the hastily drawn on Jockeys.

"Phyllis, while you rest up, this gentleman her is going to use my slave while I have this boy here service me. Bartender, you got two rooms available?"

"You're lucky, ma'am, we do. Each with fresh sheets, but I expect one hell of a tip for all this," he chuckled.

"You'll get your tip. Don't worry." With that she handed her slave's leash to Adam and Adam handed her my tit leash. The other slave, wet with sweat, looked totally defeated when he realized he was going to be fucked up his ass or down his throat, or probably both, by this total stranger.

"May I lube, master?" the slaveboy pleaded.

Adam look surprised in that all his slaves were lubed every morning routinely, but then realized that a male slave owned by a woman would probably only need lube on their prick, not their asshole.

"Any lube, bartender?" Adam asked.

"There's a tube on the table by the bed," the bartender shot back, amused. "We aim to please in this bar, sir," he laughed.

"OK, slaveboy, you can lube if that's what you want," Adam said as he jerked on the slaveboy's leash and led him to one of the back rooms.

"Thank you, master. Thank you," the handsome slave said as he hustled to the back room he had just emerged from, still reeking with the smell of sex.

I was promptly led to another back room and promptly put to work pleasuring this woman, a task I hadn't done since about the third month of my training when heterosexual services were being emphasized. Through the thin walls, I could hear my master pounding into the older lady's slave's ass as he groaned from the assault up his chute. The mistress started fucking me with me flat on my back and her on top riding my erect shaft. After a time, she shifted to her back with me fucking her face-to-face as she directed the depth, angle, and speed of each movement, constantly reminding me I did not have permission to shoot. Just as I heard my master yell out in the passion of his eruption in the next room, my mistress gasped, then contracted every muscle in her body, and finally screamed in ecstasy as one organism after another racked her body as I continued pumping deeply into her as ordered. Finally, she ordered me off of her and shakily got to her feet. The room swilled in sex smells and my need to ejaculate was overwhelming.

Without saying a word, she grabbed my leash and led me back to the bar, my prick slick with her body juices and dripping steadily with my urgent need. My body had the strong smell of sex and was covered with sweat from my exertions. Soon I was joined by her own slave, apparently in the same condition. We briefly looked at each other with a mutual recognition of how thoroughly our bodies had been exploited at the whims of our owners and how we, as slaves, could do absolutely nothing but cooperate with our own debasement. Both of us knew we were nothing but whores and probably always would be, being good looking and sexually appealing, until we were too old to be fetching where we would face an even worse life.

"He's a good fuck - well trained," Adam said to Alice.

"Your slave's a good stud," Alice replied. "Trading off was fun. We'll do it again if we ever meet up again."

"If you ever want to sell your boy, look me up," Adam said, handing her his card. "I'll give you top price."

"Thanks. I just may do that. I get bored with them after a while," Alice said sweetly.

"What your slaveboy's background?" Adam asked Alice.

"Nothing too unusual. Knocked up the 15-year-old daughter of a top government official. Got busted for exploitation of a free minor and sentenced to life-time slavery. I'm his third owner since his slave training was completed, but I understand in every case he was bought for use of his body. I'm not surprised in view of his good looks and that great body. But isn't it ironic that he was enslaved for fucking and now that's his full time job?" Alice laughed uproariously. "Who says there isn't justice in this world? Of course, it's pretty stupid to go fucking around with a 15-year-old princess of a top government man."

"That is poetic justice, Alice," Adam laughed. "But a slave looking like him could hardly expect being bought for anything not involving use of that beautiful body in one fashion or another. He's just lucky he wasn't bought up by one of those brothels where you're fucked round-the-clock."

"Well, he may be yet," Alice replied gayly. "He's just lucky so far."

The two slaves kneeling in the bar visibly shivered at the way the conversation was going because they both knew everything said was absolutely true in their world. A furtive embarrassed look into each other's eyes confirmed their mutual plight.

"Remember, Alice. First dibs on your slave when you get bored with it," Adam said as he finished his beer and, grabbing the doctor's tit leash, headed for the exit, this time directly back to the car. I was unleashed the minute I had opened the back door and appropriately knelt for my master's entry, then again rushed around to the driver's side to get the air conditioning going.

"Home, doctor," Adam ordered. "As soon as you get the car parked, come up to the sitting room. I want to fuck you again before you start your exercise regimen. Or maybe just have you suck me off - we'll decide later. Well, I know what. You suck me off first until I'm ready to go and then I'll fuck you. How does that sound, doctor?"

"Fine, master," I said. "Whatever pleases my master." They were the standard responses taught month after month in the slave training school. Now I understood how useful that training was. A slave didn't even have to think before responding after he'd been fully trained.

Sure enough, I did suck him until he was ready to orgasm and just before, he turned me over on my back and fucked me thoroughly. As soon as he shot deep into me, I was dismissed with a slap on my rump and sent to the gym for my grueling three-hour exercise program, complete with the ever-present threat of severe shocks at any sign of less than total output. By the time the steward unstrapped me from the machine, I had suffered three severe and extremely painful shocks which the steward thought was very good for a starter. When that was over, I literally crawled to the baths before starting my laundry work. I knew I would be called on again before I was caged for the night.

I got all the laundry done and was, sure enough, called back to the sitting room where Chad and another friend had arrived to visit my master. Before the evening was over, all three men had fucked me twice, and the stranger added two more after that. My ass was so sore I could barely walk as I struggled down to the baths before having the steward feed and water me and put some smoothing lotion of up my ravished asshole. After my 10 lashes with the Mylar whip for "being a slave," he motioned for me to get in my cage while I remembered to thank him profusely for my instructional beating.

"Thank you, bossman sir, for taking care of me," I said, using the correct term I had learned in my slave training to address a supervisor who was also a slave.

"I suppose you're wondering where Cofkuby is at?" the steward said quietly, looking pointedly at the empty cage next to mine."

"Yes, bossman sir," I said sleepily.

"Our master has him on loan to a business associate who is hosting a convention. He won't be back for a week or so, and," he sighed, "a little worse for wear if it's like the last time he was loaned out."

I must have looked alarmed because the steward added, "You see, the master frequently loans you boys out if there's a business advantage involved. That just makes good sense, but the problem comes in the fact that you boys often get fucked non-stop for hours on end by hundreds of people all lined up for the convention freebies. It may take Cofkuby several days to heal after he returns. In that case, doctor, you'll have to take up the slack around here."

I moaned in that I could barely move now from all the fucking I'd received upstairs.

"I know you're sore, doctor, but it'll feel better tomorrow with that ointment I put up you after your enemas. It'll prevent any infections and toughens the skin up your chute, so you can handle being fucked repeatedly a little better. I'll try to suggest to the master that he use some of the other boys over the next few days - Lord knows there are plenty of them around here for just that purpose - but you're the newest attraction and until the novelty wears off, you might as well count on a sore butt around the clock. I'll suggest the other boys, but, you know, he is the master."

"Thank you, bossman, sir. Thank you." With that, I crawled into the tiny cage, went into the only position that would hold all of me and still get the cage door shut, and went soundly asleep.

CHAPTER 6

THE STUD FARM

The steward was good for his word. The next day, he had rounded up six other slaves the master kept for his amusement and paraded each around to interest the master in what their bodies had to offer. Three of the six were black, handsome to a fault, and hung like young colts. All were around 18, were very muscular, and seemed born to be what they were - pleasure slaves. They were frisky and appeared to be interested in being used by the master as all sported constant erections and pleading seductive looks in their eyes. Thankfully, the strategy worked. The master fucked two of them and only used me to fuck the third black, who had recently had his gonads replaced with steel balls inside his original sac so he still looked the same but was now less than a full man and totally spermless.

While our owner looked on, I fucked away as ordered while he told me the story of the three black slaves. All three were half-brothers, having been sired out of the same stud on different broods in a stud farm located in New Jersey. Being born into slavery, they had never known life as anything but a slave, and had been placed up for auction as soon as they were fully grown and had completed their training when they were around 15. Adam had bought them at that time and they had been in his service for the past three years. Adam explained that they seemed to be very happy with him in that their life was exactly what they had been brought up to expect - probably a little better - and that they were always trying to find new ways for their bodies to please their owner. He had decided to castrate one of them in that he had heard castrated males offered a better fuck in that being fucked was their only way of gaining any sexual feelings at all. Consequently, they put more "heart" into being fucked and eagerly sought it out at every opportunity. But the castrator had talked him into inserting the steel balls into the sac once holding the slave's gonads so that his appearance would remain exactly the same.

"Does he fuck better, Doctor?" Adam asked as I continued pumping away.

"Seems like it," I answered cautiously. "Of course, I haven't fucked enough to draw much comparison."

"Naw - you're right. You're usually the one getting fucked, aren't you?" he laughed.

"Yes, master," I gasped between pumping into the black slave's butt.

"Except when I loan you out to my women friends," my master laughed again. "Was she a good fuck, doctor?"

"I think so, master. It's been some time since I had fucked a woman - not since my training, master."

"Well, she thought you were OK," Adam said, "and that's all that matters, isn't it?"

"Yes, master," I answered. "Master, may I shoot?" I gasped.

"No, doctor." Adam quickly replied. "I've got other plans for you today."

"Yes, master," I gasped.

"OK, pull it out. You're done for now. I've seen all the fucking I want out of you two - sort of a study of white in black," he laughed. "I want you to notice the boner on that slave you've just fucked, doctor. He loved it just as much as you did. If you nut a slave after they're full grown, they don't lose a bit of their sexual drive or stamina - just their juice. That's the only difference. Do they teach that to you in medical school?"

"No, master, not that I can recall," I answered meekly.

"Well, any slave veterinarian knows that," my master replied. "One of the first things they learn is how to nut a slaveboy."

Adam ordered the three non-black slaves back to the steward for work assignments and told me to bring his Audi station wagon around to the front. As soon as I was kneeling by the opened rear door, he brought the all three black slaves, now leashed by their neck collars but still totally nude, to the rear of the Audi and opened the tailgate, ordering them into the back compartment and then to kneel facing the rear window. When he had seated himself in the rear, he took the three leashes in his hand and held them on short leash while I ran around and got in the driver's seat.

Taking a card out of his shirt pocket, he ordered me to go out to Route 22 and head north for approximately 17 miles. When I came to William's Stud Farm, I was to turn off and head for the main office.

With 40 minutes, I was driving up in front of the main office and hurried around to open the door for my master. Kneeling, I remembered Mr. Williams was the one who had looked me over so thoroughly at the mall and had offered to buy me. I also remembered he had said he needed black studs as soon as possible to meet the demands. Were all four of us to be sold to a breeding farm? If so, why would my master have brought the castrated black with us?

After my master had gotten the three black slaves out of the back, stretching as they worked their cramps out from the close confinement, he leashed them by the neck and then came around and leashed me by my left tit ring. He entered the office with all four of us slaves in tow.

"You took me up on my offer!" Mr. William's exclaimed. "And, better yet, you've brought me the black studs I needed, you're a good man. The price I'll give for your stock will reflect just how grateful I am. Since we last met, the demand for black studs has gone even higher, and your white boy there looks even better than I remember. Yes sir, top dollar."

"Hold on, my friend," Adam said. "I'll sell you two of these black boys as studs if the price is right. One of the slaves isn't for sale - at least right now, and I don't think you'll be interested in the other black."

"Well, two's better than nothing so I'm grateful. I know the white slave is your personal attendant so I understand not selling him if you don't want, although I could sure use him here if you change your mind. But why wouldn't I want one of these black boys? They all look just about perfect from what I can see," Mr. Williams said as he swiftly swept over the black boy's bodies. "May I?" he asked Adam, reaching toward the black's huge organs.

"Of course, Mr. Williams," Adam answered.

Mr. Williams went to the first black, hefted his genitals in his palm, churned the ball sac thoroughly, and then swiftly stroked the boy until he was hard and dripping. Satisfied, he went to the next black and did the same who responded in like manner. He then moved to the third black, hefted his ball sac and began churning.

"Whoa," he said. "This boy's been nutted. Good job, though, with the ball replacement. You can't tell by looking. Steel or plastic?" he asked as he continued churning the slave's ballsac.

"Steel," Adam replied. "The vet thought the plastic balls were too light and wouldn't give him a natural hang."

"Well, he isn't worth a damn around here, although I admit he's pretty enough to buy just to fuck myself. Is that why you brought him out?" he asked.

"No," Adam laughed. "I just wanted to see how long it would take you to spot a fake stud. It took all of 10 seconds. You're good - very good. But he is a damn good fuck and I'll sell him if the price is right. Don't feel any obligation, though. I've got a lady friend that will buy him in a minute now that he can't knock her up and can fuck all night if that's what she wants."

"Shit, I need another slave around here just to fuck like I need a hole in the head. Hell, I can fuck my studs anytime I want. They don't mind - it's sort of a break for them to get fucked instead of having to fuck all the time. Let your lady friend have her fun with him - but he's a real looker, isn't he?" He said admiringly, reaching up from the slave's ball sac and pinching the ringed tits of the boy until they were fully erect. "But these other two? Do they test out fully fertile? That's essential around here," he smirked.

"Tested 100 percent with way above average sperm count and a full half-cup discharge every time these boys pop off. Born slaves, they're products of a stud farm like this and trained from birth on for a life of service. All three blacks are half-brothers - all products of the same stud. Shouldn't have a bit of trouble with them. Paid $400,000 each and I expect a profit now that they're full grown. I bought them when they were just 15 and they just turned 18. You should get a lot of service out of them before they dry up. How about $600,000 each?"

"$500,000 sounds more reasonable," Mr. Williams replied hopefully.

"$560,000 a piece and they're yours. You can have them studding within the hour."

"It's a deal," Mr. Williams said with a handshake. "And I probably will put them to stud before the sun sets. The demand for black sperm is really high right now. Now, you want to sell hat white boy - like I said, he'd make a damn fine stud too, if his lab tests are OK."

"He tests out 100% fertile so no problems there, but he's getting along - he's in his early 30s now and doesn't have too many years left if put to stud around the clock. I've only had him a short time and haven't really broken him in yet to my routine. I think I'll keep him. Besides, I need a chauffeur to get home," Adam laughed, "especially since I have to haul the castrated black back with me. No, I primarily brought this white property out in that I thought you might enjoy fucking him. You so admired him at the mall the other day. It's on me - a little gift for buying my excess properties."

"That's damn nice of you," Mr. Williams said "I'll just take you up on that - is right now OK?"

"Here's his leash," Adam chucked. "Enjoy."

"Well, while I'm playing around, why don't I have my steward take these two new boys back to the breeding barns and you can look around and see the operation for yourself."

"Great!" Adam responded. "I'd enjoy that - I've never seen a breeding farm in operation."

Instantly, Mr. William snapped his finger and his slave steward stepped out of the shadows, a magnificent mulatto dressed only in his neck collar, genital band, and a Mylar whip as well as the standard leather slave whip fastened to a belt around his naked waist. He took the leashes of the two newly purchased black slaves in one hand, fastened the leash of their castrated half-brother to a retaining ring in the office with his other hand, and, bowing deeply, asked me to follow him to the breeding barns where it would be his privilege to show me around. The three blacks, together since birth as half-brothers, realized their castrated brother had not been sold with them and that they would probably never see him again. As they were led away, they looked wistfully at the unsold brother, saying goodbye with their eyes. The castrated black's eyes welled up as he took a last look at his brothers, now being tugged by their leashes by their new steward. All three knew had known separation was eventually inevitable as slaves and they had been fortunate to remain together as long as they had. Such were the realities of slavery.

About three blocks behind the office was the core of the operation: the breeding barns. They were spacious and airy with good ventilation and scrupulously clean. You could have eaten off the floor. Located at intervals throughout the barn were deeply padded sawhorses of varying heights with shackles reaching out from all four legs. Interspersed among the sawhorses were padded low benches, again with shackles appropriately positioned to handle a variety of ankle and wrist lengths. Most of the benches also had waist straps with small pillows, gags, blindfolds, lubricant dispensers, first aid cream, disposable tissues, and other accouterments on a shelf underneath. The equipment clearly bespoke the purpose of the building.

Around two sides of the buildings were barred cages holding the available studs. Each cage was fully open on the side facing the interior so that the owner purchasing his service could get a good view of his body through the bars (of course, most owners insisted on a full body inspection outside the cage before closing the deal). Attached to the open bars was a small placard listing the stud's body dimensions, his age, his genetic origins, his slave history (bred or freeborn; if freeborn, years in slavery; number of owners; major assigned duties in previous ownerships; etc.); years in stud service, and number of "hits" or successful breeding's to date, as well as information of success in impregnating on a first mating, a second mating, etc. Also listed were the number of multiple births resulting from his stud services; number of defective births; and any special considerations, e.g., size of organ so big it might tear a brood slave with a small vagina. Each of the studs wore only a neck collar: tit rings would only get in the way of breeding it was thought; and genital rings might interfere with full penetration occasionally. Nose rings and earrings were similarly disallowed in that it was thought some broods, in the height of passion, might tear at them in addition to the ever present danger of scratching the stud's backs - a danger very evident in the many scratches on most of the stud's backs. All in all, there were 24 cages; 16 of which held occupants at the time.

"Four of them are on duty right now," the steward explained when he saw me counting the number of unoccupied cages. "These two new purchases will leave us only two empty cages for future purchases. The studs are always caged separately. We don't want any fooling around with each other - all their sap has got to be saved for their assigned stud duties."

I expected him to cage the two newly purchased blacks right then and there, but, instead, he led them over to an aged slave in a fittings shop over to one side. "Jake, here's two new studs. Take their tit rings and genital bands off - they won't be needing those for a while."

"Yes, sir, bossman," the old slave promptly replied. Without further ado, he reached for some heavy iron snips with a long levered handle and quickly removed both bands and all four tit rings. Both of the slaves' genitals were suddenly free to hang loose once again and the feel of free swinging balls felt strange to the slaves, changing their center of gravity slightly.

"It's OK, boys," the steward assured them. "You'll get used to hanging loose soon enough and those sore tits that are bleeding a little from the rings being removed will be fine in a day or so." That said he grabbed a tube of first aid cream the blacksmith keep handy and rubbed it on their bleeding tits and where the genital band had been. "Don't worry - your tits will still stay plenty big, but they will shrink a little from when they were ringed. They'll never get down to the size they were before you were ringed."

"Yes sir, bossman," the two slaves said, staring at each other's breeding tits and the red mark on their shaft where the genital band had continually rubbed.

Tugging on their leashes, he led each to a spotlessly clean cage and, taking a tape measure, carefully measured each of them, including their penis at full erection. He then locked them in, asking them a few questions after they were safely caged and he no longer had to leash them.

"Did your owner say you were 18?"

"Yes, bossman sir."

"Are you really 18 or was he exaggerating a bit."

"No, bossman sir, we just turned 18."

"You full black as far as you know?"

"Yes, bossman, sir - we were bred at a place like this to make sure we were pure breeds."

"How many owners you boys had so far?"

"Just two so far, bossman sir. The master that just sold us got us at auction from the stud farm where we were raised."

"What did he use you for mainly - you just fuckboys primarily?"

"Yes sir, bossman sir. That's what he bought us for - mainly. Of course, we did gardening and plenty of hard housework too when he wanted. We also waited tables for him and his guests."

"Your first owner - what did he use you for - primarily?"

"He's the one that raised us for market. Spent most of our time being trained as houseboys and fuck slaves.

"Bossman, sir, can I ask a question, sir?" one of the black slaves humbly asked.

"As long as it's brief and to the point, slave. We don't take to slaves talking much. That's not what you're here for."

"Yes sir, Bossman. I just wondered if we were going to be studs now, like on the breeding farm we were raised on."

"That's what you're going to be all right, both of you. Lucky bastards! You're going to get to fuck your hearts out day and night and if you don't it's my job to motivate you properly," he said reaching for his Mylar whip. "Studs that don't cooperate fully don't last long," he added darkly. "We either, beat them to death, starve them to death, or sell them off to the mines where they never see anything but the end of a whip the rest of their lives. Even if you hated studding, anything's better than the mines."

"Yes sir, bossman sir. That's what I thought," the black slave who had asked the question responded. "Thank you, bossman sir."

There was a long pause. Finally, the steward's leather whip slashed across the bars of the cage. "Well, you bastards, is that it?"

Both of the caged slaves looked terrified, not knowing how to respond.

"Aren't you going to tell me how good a stud you're going to me under my tutelage, you worthless sons-of-bitches or shall we start beating you to death right now?"

"Yes sir, Yes sir, bossman. We're going to be good studs. You won't be needing to whip us, bossman, sir. We'll be humping just like you want any time you want, bossman sir. We sure like studding better than being fucked all the time, bossman sir."

"That's more like it," the steward said, meaningfully folding his whip but not replacing it in his belt. "Remember, if I'm disappointed in any way, you'll feel it across your back and rump until you wish you were dead, stud boys. I'm glad you think you'll like studding, but remember, you're still going to get your asses fucked now and then. Both your new owner, the slave handlers, and I take our pleasure with the studs whenever we get a chance and we expect you studs to take a strong interest in giving us maximum pleasure any way we want it when you're lucky enough to catch our attention," he added rather threateningly.

"Yes sir, bossman. We'll pleasure you and the master good anytime you want," the two new slaves chorused. "That's where we're most experienced right now, bossman, sir."

"Yes, so I've heard." That said, the steward took a marker and began filling out the placard on the front of each of the newly-occupied cages:

AGE: 18

BODY DIMENSIONS: Neck 18"; Chest 46"; Waist 33"; Hips 45"; Penis (Erect): 9x5"

GENETIC BACKGROUND: Full black from healthy disease-free breeding stock

SLAVERY BACKGROUND: Bred slave - no history of free status

NUMBER OF OWNERS: Three (including present owner).

PREVIOUS MAJOR ASSIGNED DUTIES: Houseboy and personal fuck boy.

YEARS IN STUD SERVICE: Newly acquired

STUD RECORD: Unknown at this time. Tested 100% fertile with well above average sperm count and seminal output.

That done, he turned to me and said apologetically, "I'm sorry, master, that I had to get them caged before I could take you on a tour of our facilities, but I'm sure you didn't want to bother with them now that they're sold. Now that you're seen the cages and the little fittings shop we have here, let me show you the actual operations, master."

CHAPTER 7

BREESDING OPPERATIONS

That said, the steward courteously led me back to the center of the room, and rang a bell. Instantly, two slave handlers brought in a middle-aged female slave, totally naked, with obvious stretch marks on her belly indicating numerous pregnancies before. She was crying but no one paid any attention as she was unceremoniously strapped across a padded sawhorse until her vagina was exposed and open due to her legs being chained far apart. Her wrists were short-chained to the forward legs of the sawhorse so her head was forced far below her exposed organs. Once firmly secured, the two handlers, slaves themselves, quickly headed for the cage area and returned with a magnificently built white slave who looked to be in his early 20s led by a leash connected to his slave collar. He had golden hair, blue eyes, an exceptionally long, thick shaft already quivering in hard readiness, and beautiful smooth skin covered with just a faint coating of shimmering blonde body hair. Obviously, there was no need to body shave this boy except around his genitals, which were shaved as smooth as a baby's to assure absolute cleanliness. One of the handlers greased the blonde slave's shaft from an attached jar of lubricant until he was fully hard and completely covered in the germicidal lubricant.

"Go to it, 12," one of the slave handlers unceremoniously commanded, raising his whip.

"Yes, bossman sir," the stud slave responded in a matter of fact manner as he promptly plunged full length into the slave woman's vagina and began vigorously pumping his shaft in and out of her as she first gasped, then moaned.

After a minute or so, the slave handler rather lightly smacked the stud on his ass with the leather slave whip urging him to pump a little faster and to get his shaft in the woman as far as he could. The slave promptly delved even deeper into the woman and increased his pace until he was panting profusely with his efforts. The woman beneath him cried piteously but eventually relaxed enough to at least tolerate the fucking by the handsome stud without crying out, although she was never allowed to actually look at him directly. His large organ hurt her too much to allow much enjoyment, however, and it felt like he was going to split her in half before he was through with her. Every stud she'd be put to all had these huge organs that stretched her so much the pain was practically unbearable. Soon, the slave handler reached down and grabbed the stud slave's balls, squeezing them rather sharply.

"He's about ready to shoot, steward, sir," the slave handler informed the steward.

"Good. Keep your hands on his balls so you know when he's shooting and just at that moment give him a good smack on his butt with the handle of your whip. That little jolt with the whip makes sure the stud empties his balls completely and isn't holding back on us," he informed the handler.

"Yes sir, bossman, sir," the handler replied, reading his whip handle with this left hand while his right hand squeezed the stud's balls tightly.

Within 30 seconds, the stud gasped as the first eruption was deposited deep within the woman slave beneath him just as the whip handle smashed across his rear, driving him even deeper into the woman for his second, third, fourth, and fifth eruptions.

"Feels like he's emptied now, bossman sir," the slave handler announced, giving the stud's balls one last squeeze to prove his point.

"OK, order the stud to pull out, have him clean his prick and balls with those antiseptic wipes we keep right here for his convenience, and get him back in his cage to rest up. I think we have him scheduled for two more breedings today."

"Yes sir, bossman, sir" the handler said as he jerked on the stud's collar as a signal for him to withdraw from the woman he had serviced, pointed to the antiseptic wipes which the stud promptly cleaned himself with, and then, with another jerk to his collar, led him back to his cage. "Good job, 12. Good job," we heard the slave handler say to the stud as he was locking him back in his cage. "Now you concentrate on getting those balls of yours full again. You're got two more to do today and so far, you haven't earned any demerits. Let's keep it that way so the steward won't have to have you beaten again tonight with the Mylar whip for further instruction."

"Yes sir, bossman, yes sir," we heard the handsome, blonde slave, obviously named after his cage number, respond. "No need to beat this stud slave, bossman. He'll fuck those slave women good and proper so they're all knocked up first time around."

"That's what we expect out of you, 12 - each and every time. But, 12, you're going to get beaten - it's just a question of how much and how often. Don't forget you're just a slave, 12, and have a lot to learn," the handler warned.

"No sir, bossman, sir. This slave deserves a beating if the bossmen decide that's what he needs, bossman sir," 12 promptly reassured his handler he understood the necessity of disciplinary beatings for a slave.

The steward was amused at the chatter between the handler and the spent stud and smiled as he overheard their conversation, obviously satisfied with both of their performances. Turning to me again, he asked, "Would you like to see the studding done in the face to face position?"

"Why not?" I responded. "I imagine your owner will need the time to take full advantage of the slaveboy I loaned him for his pleasure."

"I'm sure he's most grateful, master," the steward smoothly replied. He rang another bell and again, a woman, totally nude, was brought forward by the two slave handlers and strapped to one of the low benches dominating the center of the barn. She was then fitted with a blindfold and a gag as well as having a broad belt strapped around her middle. When I looked questioningly, the steward explained.

"We don't want the females knowing which stud their owner picked out for them - jealously, you know - besides it's none of their business if their owner wants to put a donkey to them - so we blindfold them. We gag them so they don't bite our studs on the nipples or anywhere else. We don't care if they scream, but the biting damages our property. The belt around the middle is to prevent them buckling when the studs are really pounding into them. Before we learned to buckle them down tightly, we sometimes had them bending their backs so much they were practically throwing those big studs right off of them. Properly controlled, it makes it easy for our studs to fuck them properly, no matter what their attitude is about it."

The steward's point was well made. The woman, about 23, screamed as she was drug in by the two brutish slave handlers, screamed even louder as she was strapped down to the four corners of the bench, bellowed in agony as a pillow was placed under her and then was strapped tightly to the bench forcing her vagina into a protruding position, and shrieked as the blindfold was strapped around her head and then her head was harnessed and also strapped to the bench. The only thing that shut her up was when the gag was forced in her mouth, a move firmly resisted until one of the handler's held her nose shut until she was forced to open her mouth. The minute she did, she was gagged once and for all with the strap holding it firmly attached to her head harness.

The steward laughed, pointing out that some women liked being fucked so much they bought stud slaves just for that purpose. In fact, some of the studs they had owned here at this very farm were sold just for that purpose as their sperm count decreased. Why this stupid slave was putting on such a show was beyond him. Left to her own devices, she could hardly attract anything approaching the handsome, well-equipped studs that would service her here.

Properly silenced, the slave handlers went back to the cages and brought forth another beautiful specimen of manhood leashed by his collar and obviously ready for the occasion judging by his dripping erect shaft. This stud was a Latino about 6′ tall, extremely muscular, and absolutely hairless except for his dark curly head hair. He had only needed to be body shaved in his genital area. His skin was a golden tan and his face was about as handsome as men get, highlighted by flashing black eyes, thick black eyelashes, and a pencil line beard outlining his jawline.

"8 here hasn't been used yet today and he's eager, I see," the steward said, pointing to the slave's dripping shaft. "When a slave's put to stud four or five times a day, sometimes even more around here, it doesn't take long to where they're producing so much spunk that if you don't drain them frequently, they take to leaking all over the place. It's quite a mess in their cages if you let that happen. So, if no one requests them, we milk them on a rigid schedule just to keep their cages nice and clean and to make sure they keep up their sperm production. This stud hasn't been drained in over 12 hours now and you can see he's about frantic with need. That happens after you've been a stud here for a few months being drained regularly."

Without further ado, 8 quickly mounted the woman and ramped his prick in full length in the first stroke. He promptly began pumping wildly; seeming to enjoy feeling the captive body squirm and jerk beneath him as he thoroughly fucked her. Within a minute or so, he felt his handler's hand on his balls and knew he'd be smacked smartly just when he orgasmed. Within seconds, the first volley shot forth as his ass checks were smacked with the whip handle, and he emptied totally into the woman writhing beneath him.

"Maschismo, steward, sir?" the slave said as he withdrew his huge shaft from the now swollen vagina, acknowledging the two of us observing his performance...

"Yes, 8, you are maschismo in a big way. That's why the master bought you," the steward said. "Keep up your maschismo and your handler won't need to beat you so often."

"Thank you, steward, sir, thank you," the Latino stud answered with sincere gratitude.

After cleaning himself off with the antiseptic wipes, he was led back to his cage, obviously happy to have been allowed to relieve his great need. We heard his handler compliment him on his performance and promising him that, if he were good and could attract another purchaser of his services, that he would be allowed to cum again.

"Thank you, bossman, sir, thank you," the Latino stud replied as he entered his cage without prompting.

"Do all the slave women resist being bred like this?"

"No, master. It's only about one in five, I'd say. Those 20 % have to be strapped down and raped like you just saw; the other 80% look forward to a good fucking with a handsome stud. It's about the only sex most of them ever get as slaves and they relish their short time on the bench. We generally don't need to restrain them in any way and generally let them get fucked any way they want, master. We call them "back scratchers" because they're the ones that scratch our studs backs up in the height of passion, master," the steward explained.

"Which do the studs like better - the 'back scratchers' or the ones they just rape?"

"Some like the 'back scratchers;' some like the ones they just rape. Depends on the stud, master. They know they don't have any choice in the matter and are going to have to stud regardless, master, but still, I think they like the variety. I suppose it even depends on their mood at the moment, master, but, who knows? The studs know voicing their feelings or opinions only leads to severe punishment, master, as it would, of course, for any slave, not just these studs here, so what their mood is or isn't is of no consequence and they know it. Overall, I would say most of them like the variety - a few willing and a few not-so-willing, master - but all our studs here do what they're told regardless or suffer severe consequences, so it doesn't really matter."

"Well, that make's sense. All of us like a little variety in our lives," I commented.

"My master uses some of the studs for his own pleasure and he lets me use them as a special privilege as the slave steward, master, so they all get a little more variety that way too. I used that blonde stud you just saw in action last night, master, so being fucked instead of doing the fucking offered him a change of pace, master. Of course, he didn't have any choice in the matter, but he gave no indication he didn't appreciate the variety in his usage, master."

"Do any of the stud slaves object to studding?"

"In all the time I've been steward, I've only seen two or three studs give us any trouble in being ordered to rape the slave women sent here for impregnation who are resistant, but some swift and memorable beatings stopped that nonsense, master. As I recall, master, their objection wasn't to raping the women - it was some philosophical nonsense about being used to make new slaves. When they were faced with fucking or not eating, they came to their senses real fast. Nevertheless, the master ordered instructional thrashings so they would remember what they did wasn't any of their business, let alone a slave's choice. After their severe beating and a night without food, they forgot all about it and got on with their work, master. They weren't too bright as I recall - they seemed to have forgotten why the master had bought them to start with," he laughed.

"Well, I would think. Never heard of such nonsense, especially from a slave," I added.

Meanwhile, the other handler slowly took the restraints off of the thoroughly fucked woman but left the gag in place until she was back in her cage. The steward said that was standard procedure so there was no chance they could bite the handlers. They would only be returned to their owners when they were guaranteed pregnant which might take a few sessions despite the fact they were only breed when they were in their peak period of fertility each month. If they still weren't impregnated after that three or four day period, they were returned to their owners and rescheduled for the next month. Generally, an owner didn't have to pay a stud fee until his slave was pregnant unless repeated attempts proved the slave had reached total infertility due to old age or other factors. Most female slaves were bred from the time they were 17 or so until they couldn't be impregnated any more, usually around 40 to 42. By then, they had generally be able to produce 20-22 new slaves if they had been scheduled properly for maximum production and if they had been mated with fully fertile males with high rates of impregnation during their peak periods of insemination. Slave husbandry was a most profitable business and few owners treated it lightly if they wanted a good return on their investment. Since female slaves could be worked at least eight of the nine months of their pregnancies, their productivity didn't suffer too much from their constant pregnancies which were viewed as an excellent source of secondary income. Most owners didn't bother buying the studs themselves - after all, one stud could cover hundreds of females - so renting a stud's services was rather routine, especially for the small slaveholder (one with less than a 1000 or so slaves). Since few studs were actually needed considering the numbers of females serviced, owners could afford to select only those with almost perfect physiques, exceptional good looks, excellent health and musculature, high degrees of disease resistance, and massive genitals which could get the job done. No one believed anymore that big genitals meant high fertility rates, but everyone knew that if you could produce a slave with big genitals it meant a big bonus when it came to selling the commodity in that most owners preferred slaves very well-equipped. Therefore, available studs invariably met these specifications. It was thought their male offspring would probably be as well-endowed as their genetic fathers and that their female offspring would probably breed male children similarly equipped. To date, this careful slave husbandry had paid off: the bred slave population was significantly bigger, better built, better equipped, considerably better looking, more disease resistant, and more easily sexually aroused than the non-bred slave population by a large margin. Therefore, bred slaves generally brought considerably more money at auction time, especially since they had usually been trained since birth to their slave status - an adjustment requiring a lot of intensive and lengthy training when converting a free person to slave status. If the trend kept up, it was estimated eventually most slaves would be bred to specification with only criminals, social deviants, and other undesirables being left for the intensive slave-training institutes to cope with. Already some people were clamoring to get legislation requiring all male slaves not bred be castrated in the slave-training institutes before being auctioned so they didn't contaminate the gene pool of slaves if they ever got a chance to breed. Others thought this was totally unnecessary in view of the fact that few slaves were ever allowed to procreate without their owner's express permission which was rarely granted if the slave showed any genetic defects or was uncomely in any way.

"Well, master, that's about it. Do you suspect my master is through using your slave?" he politely asked.

"Probably. We better get back. Your operation is interesting. I can see why so many people choose the services you offer. But I haven't seen all of the studs you offer yet."

"Master," the steward paled, "I'm so sorry. I simply forgot. How stupid of me. Please tell my master so he can order a correctional beating or perhaps you would like me to do so?"

"You won't need to do that - I'll tell him," I said firmly, not letting some slave manipulate me so blatantly.

The steward bit his lip and quickly led me to the rest of the cages.

"We're in between actual studdings right at this moment," the steward explained, "so I can show you all our stock."

We proceeded to view all the studs. Some, mistaking me for a buyer of their services, stuck their universally gigantic organs through the bars of the cages and begged me to buy them to stud my female slaves. When I raised my eyebrows at such portentous action, the steward explained the studs were usually beaten as well as denied food and water if they didn't actively solicit their usage. Mr. Wilson had every conceivable type of human male available for stud with the exception they were all extremely good looking, all were big and muscular, and all sported huge balls and penises. You could pick from Italians, Germans, Swedish blondes, Latinos, blacks, Asians, mulattos, Greeks, Arabs - you name it. Almost anything seemed available. Most of the studs were fully erect as we looked them over, most were dripping in need, most seemed shameless in soliciting their usage as studs, and every one of them seemed totally acclimated to their ownership by others for this purpose. Not one looked rebellious, sullen, resentful, embarrassed, or despondent. Quite the contrary. Most looked eager to get to their work and, when picked out for inspection, happily cooperated in the inspection of their body by potential buyers of their services. I was glad I had sold the two black boys to Mr. Wilson. It was obvious they were going to enjoy their new role after their initial adjustment if the studs I looked over were any example. It was also obvious Mr. Wilson and his steward took good care of the stock. All looked healthy, well fed, and ready to go. One or two looked haggard at the moment, but the steward pointed out they had been used heavily over the past 24 hours and would be put to rest for 8 hours or so until they recovered.

"What do you call heavy use, steward," I asked.

"More than five times within a 24-hour period, master. Some can do more, but most get somewhat worn out when you go beyond the magic five. Of course, master, as they age, we have to get down to four a day and if they have trouble with that, we just sell them and replace them with fresh stock."

"How long does a stud last here then?"

"Most about four or five years, master. After that, they begin to have trouble getting aroused and when that happens, we just sell them off, master."

"Who buys them?" I queried.

"Mainly middle-aged women looking for an experienced male slave, master. It makes a perfect choice in many cases in that the slave can easily satisfy the woman's needs any way she wants in that few women want to be fucked more than two or three times a day. That's nothing to most of our studs, even after years of service here. Besides, they're already trained to take commands during the fucking, so the mistress gets exactly what she wants and is usually more than satisfied. My master tries to sell our worn out studs to that market, master, if he possibly can. We also find a ready market among masters who prefer experienced men for their amusement, especially male slaves well-equipped, able to take full instructions in this area, and who are exceedingly good looking, master. Most of the studs don't mind being sold for such usage, master, in that it's a relief to be fucked instead of doing the fucking most of the time. Of course, master, some gentlemen buy our stock to fuck them on command, just like the ladies, but, again, master, the demands are usually far less than they experience here so they're happy with being sold to that destiny also. No matter who buys them, the studs are usually well pleased with their new owners in so far as they are still being bought for their sexual usage primarily. After studding for years, master, it has become part of you and you sort of think of yourself, apparently, as being born for that purpose. At least, master, that's the way I felt about it after being a stud myself for five years. Since my master chose to keep me here as the steward rather than sell me off, I still can take my pleasure with the studs when I want so it keeps me sexually drained."

"You'll enjoy those two new blacks your master bought off of me," I noted. "They're a delight to fuck."

"Thank you for suggesting that, master," the steward said rather lustily. "Of course, the master would have to approve my usage of his property first. I'm not allowed to do anything, naturally, that would interfere with the primary purpose of my master's operation."

"Oh, I imagine he'll let you fuck them as long as they're not allowed to shoot off. That's not going to hurt them one bit in terms of them studding."

"Yes, master," the steward said.

"How many handlers do you need?" I asked.

"We only need about four of those types of slaves usually unless it's a very busy season. Normally, there's only one studding or so going on at any given time and each studding just takes two handlers, so even if we schedule two at once, four handlers are plenty. When they aren't needed in the actual studding operations, they administer the food, water, discipline beatings, and cleanliness inspections the stud slaves require around the clock. Of course, the studs are required to keep their own cages spotless, their bodies equally clean at all times, body shaved as necessary, and to report any ailments whatsoever, such as pulled groins, infections, etc. But they also have to be exercised regularly to keep those beautiful physiques in perfect shape so that takes a lot of the handlers' time. But four can handle it if they're worked hard - that's my job," the steward added. "Slaves are always happier if they're worked hard in my opinion, master, if my endless babble doesn't offend you."

"No, not really, but I will report your oversight of inspecting the studs to your owner," I replied.

"Of course, master," the steward replied with lowered eyes.

With that, we returned to the main office where my black slave was still chained by his collar kneeling on the floor and my doctor slave, wet with sweat, stinking of sex, and looking rather used, was chained right next to him.

"Thanks for the treat," Mr. Wilson said cheerily to my owner. "He was as good in bed as I thought he might be."

"Any problems with him," I said threateningly so the doctor could overhear me. "If so, I'll enjoy beating some sense into him."

"No problems," Mr. Wilson said. "He did everything I wanted and then some. Did you steward give you a good tour?"

"It was a good tour, although I had to remind him to show me the caged studs," I answered pleasantly. "I only mention it because I'm sure you'll want to discipline him for that oversight."

"Thanks for telling me, Adam. You bet he'll be disciplined and I can guarantee you he'll never do it again. Discipline around here is something a slave remembers."

"I will say you run a very efficient operation here and the stock you have available for studding is outstanding - what a choice you give a person, and each one of them a magnificent specimen in their own right. I was particularly impressed with their eagerness to perform their duties."

"Glad to hear your evaluation, Adam. It means a lot of me and I hope you can see now why I wanted those two black boys of yours. You probably noticed I only had one full black available for stud and he's getting pretty worn out. Those two of yours meet all the requirements and my prediction is they'll take to their new life with a penchant."

"I don't doubt it. Those boys love to fuck and they've always been in a state of perpetual arousal since I've owned them. Maybe here they'll finally get it out of their system."

"I doubt it, Adam," Mr. Wilson laughed. "Some boys were just born to fuck and those former slaves of yours are probably two of them. Well, rest assured, they have a good home here as long as they can produce. After that, well, there's always the ladies and gentlemen's market."

"Yes, your steward informed me of the good aftermarket for your properties. Enjoyed it, Mr. Wilson, but I've got to get back to town. I've promised one of my friends use of the slave you just enjoyed and I plan on fucking the castrated black on the way home if I can get the seats on the Audi to fold up right."

"Doctor," Adam ordered as he undid the short chain from my leash. "Get the Audi up front here with the back seats folded down on one side. Then place this black slave face side down with his legs spread so I can fuck him easily."

"Yes, master," the doctor quickly responded, hurrying off to do his master's bidding, although it was obviously in his walk he had a mighty sore ass from his recent fucking by Mr. Wilson.

When Mr. Wilson and Adam saw the doctor's tortured walk, they both burst out in laughter.

"You must have fucked him soundly," my master laughed.

"Yes, indeed, Adam. A fuck he'll remember for some time."

As they were speeding home, the doctor heard his master fuck the black slave rather thoroughly himself. By the time they were home, the doctor had to help the black slave, crying and moaning, up from the carpeted floor and get him to his pen in that he was temporarily unable to walk. The steward commented that he was used to this and the black slave would be fine in the morning. Despite all that had gone on that day, the steward remembered to thrash the doctor five times with the Mylar whip for "being a slave." He congratulated the doctor on being a good slave that day or he would have been ordered to whip him considerably longer. By now, the doctor was used to be being beaten at least one a day and the five lashes every evening, although extremely painful, were expected and routine. Many nights, however, the doctor had displeased his master one way or another and was beaten into near unconsciousness. Such was part of being a slave, the steward reminded the doctor stoically, and the degree or severity of punishment was correctional if nothing else when you were a slave. The steward was right about the black slave's recovering - by the next morning he seemed to suffer only a very sore ass from the thorough fucking he had received from his owner the previous afternoon on the way back from the stud farm. It was a good thing in view of what transpired the next day.

CHAPTER 8

BACK TO THE DEALERS

"Adam," the soft voice cooed over the phone, "Alice here - you remember, the lady with the 20-year-old male slave whose use I traded for using your slaveboy a few weeks ago in the bar?"

"Yes, Alice, so good to hear from you. Your slaveboy was fun to fuck and I assume you had some fun with my slave as well. What's up?" Adam asked.

"You interested in trading permanently?" Alice got right to the point. "I'm getting a little bored with the boy beautiful and you asked me to call you if I ever wanted to sell my slaveboy."

"Glad you called, Alice. Could you believe I was just getting ready to call you with a proposition?" Adam laughed. "I've run across a boy for you even better than the doctor slave I let you use that afternoon. That slave was well into his 30s, you know, and would probably wear out pretty fast once you put him to proper use. This new slave, though, is perfect. He's just 18, breathtakingly handsome with a smooth black skin on him, built like Adonis, and hung like a horse. I just sold both his half-brothers as breeders but saved this one for you, Alice. I've had him castrated recently, but he's totally intact - his balls are packed with steel balls - so you don't ever have to worry about him impregnating you or your friends and, better yet, he never experiences a debilitating orgasm. You can fuck this boy all night and he'll stay hard the entire time. He's so damn muscular and big no one will ever know the boy's been cut and the slave vet did an excellent job of sewing his balls back up - you can't even see a scar. He's as good looking as that boy you've got - only this one's a shiny black with a nice smooth skin warm to the touch - you'll love him. I just sold his two brothers off as studs for $560,000 each."

"God Almighty," Alice exclaimed. "That's one hell of a price for slavemeat! Forget it if you want that much for this new blackboy - I can't afford anything that expensive, no matter what the hell he looks like."

"Calm down, Alice. I'll trade him even for the slaveboy you're getting bored with. After all, he's a real looker too and we both know he knows how to pleasure a man as well as a woman. If I recall, he was expensive when you bought him and I'm trading you a slaveboy whose worth even more - you'll be making money on this trade, Alice, if you ever decide to sell the black. If you don't like the black, I'll buy him back from you for what you paid for that stud you've currently got. It's a no-lose situation."

"Sounds like an offer I can't refuse," Alice laughed. "Tell you what; let's meet down at Goldsmith & Barnes with our two slaves. That way, if we decide to trade, all the ownership and transfer papers can be drawn up and notarized on the spot. If we decide not to trade, we can put our slaves up for auction with the dealer."

"Fine with me, Alice," Adam replied. "About noon OK? That way, if we decide not to trade, we can enter our slavemeat in the 1 PM afternoon auction and save ourselves another trip."

"See you at noon sharp over at Goldsmith & Barnes - I'll meet you in the auction barn - they're won't be anyone there yet other than the slaves up for auction being readied back in the holding pens. We'll pretty well have the place to ourselves."

"Auction Barn, 12 Noon sharp, Goldsmith & Barnes," Adam repeated. "See you there - and remember to bring your ownership papers."

"Don't worry, I always carry them with me - you never know when a sales opportunity might crop up," Alice said cheerily as she hung up.

Adam put the phone down and called for his steward.

"Steward, get the castrated black cleaned up inside and out and give him a fresh body shave. I'm going to take him down to Goldsmith & Barnes - if all goes well, he'll be fucking his new lady owner by midafternoon. Quite a switch from always being the one getting fucked around here. He might like it once he adjusts," he chuckled. "And get the doctor slave all cleaned up and polished also - he can chauffeur us to the auction barn. Tell him to bring the Cadillac around at 11 AM. We can put the castrated black in the trunk."

"Yes, master," the steward humbly replied. "Should they be clothed in any way, master?"

"No, steward. The usual: bare-ass naked. They'd only look out of place where we're going if they had anything on. And while you're getting those two ready, send up that Italian boy I bought a few weeks ago. He can fix my coffee and I think I'll cream it with his juices - café au lait. I haven't milked the boy for several days now - should be a big output by now."

"I'll send the boy up immediately, master," the steward replied promptly. "Shall I shave him first?"

"Yes, steward, but be quick about it," Adam said, dismissing the steward with his hand.

Within minutes, the young Italian slave appeared still shiny wet from his body shave. He was a stunning lad with a chiseled face highlighted by a thin beard outlining his jaw, beautiful black eyes with heavy lashes, a well-proportioned but very muscular body for one so young defined by puffy pecs, a ridged abdomen highlighting a very thin waist, huge muscular thighs below a bubble butt, and a long, very thick erect circumcised shaft atop prominent bulging balls tightly banded. His skin was baby smooth, olive colored, and totally without imperfections of any type.

"You wanted me, master?" the slave asked lustily, running his tongue languidly over his pouting lips as he thrust his pelvis forward ever so suggestively. It was obvious the slave was in a state of need and would do anything to gain some relief if his master so allowed.

"Yes, boy. Get me a fresh cup of coffee and when you return, don't kneel beside me but stand with your legs wide apart. You're going to be the 'au lait' part of the coffee this morning."

"Yes, master," the Italian slave said happily as he quickly left to get the coffee, instinctively knowing relief was imminent.

Within seconds, he was back and positioned his body as instructed beside his seated master, holding the cup of steaming coffee about a foot in front of his pelvis, already thrust outward for his master's usage. Quickly, he felt his balls being hefted up for weighing and then kneaded to test for fullness. Then he felt his master grip his shaft (it was too big for his master to get his hand all the way around it) and start pumping the huge organ. Within a minute, the slave felt the juices within him racing up his shaft with great urgency.

"Master, I'm going to shoot, master," the Italian gasped.

"Yes, slave. Make sure you shoot your whole load into the cup. You'll get beaten if you spill even one drop, slave."

"Yes master," the slave gasped as the first load literally shot into the steaming coffee, followed by spurt after spurt as his balls rapidly emptied under his master's steady pumping of his shaft. Soon the last load had found its way into the cup and the slave's legs slightly buckled as he broke out in a sex sweat.

"You completely empty, slave?" Adam asked as he continued to pump the shaft.

"Yes, master," the slaveboy gasped. "Thank you, master."

Adam reached down and felt the balls, now spongy and soft. "Feels like you emptied them out," he commented as he squeezed the balls one last time and then released the slave. "Now stir you cum into the coffee until it's frothy and then set the cup on the table here so I can enjoy it."

"Yes, master," the sweaty slave said as he quickly took the spoon and whipped the coffee into a light tan consistency, taking in the scent of the fresh coffee now flavored with hot cum. When he put the concoction on the table as ordered, he quickly sank to his knees with his knees wide spread and his head bowed, the standard slave position when not performing some commanded duty.

Adam drank the coffee down quickly, smacked his lips when finished, and announced he wanted another cup. The Italian slave sprung upward to meet the command and again returned with a second steaming cup of coffee and again assumed the position best suited for 'milking' him.

"You jerk yourself off this time right into the cup, slave. I'm tired of playing around with you right now."

"Yes, master, thank you, master" the slave answered as he quickly wrapped his hand around his own shaft and began to pump vigorously while pinching his ringed nipples with his other hand for additional stimulation. This time, it took considerably longer to produce an ejaculation, but produce he did, albeit not of the quantity of the first. Still gasping, he quickly whipped his cum into the coffee and again sank to his knees, remembering to thank his master once again for offering him another opportunity to relieve his almost chronic need. When first enslaved, the handsome Italian boy objected to anyone even touching him, let alone milking him at their whim. Now, fully acclimated to his slave status, the slave thought nothing of offering his body up for whatever purpose his master deemed - after all, his body was the property of his owner to do with as he desired. If an owner wanted to milk him of his cream, so be it - it certainly was a master's privilege. A slave had no right to object in any way - his past actions seemed so silly now in retrospect.

As Adam finished his second coffee and read the paper, the Italian slave wondered if his owner would fuck him when he was finished reading. This was the usual procedure and this morning proved to be no different. Ordered to bend over one of the sofa arms and expose his ass, the Italian boy was reamed thoroughly with this master's large prick in a long, languid fuck which took at least 30 minutes before he felt his master discharge load after load deep into his ass while he remembered to clinch his ass muscles to allow his user the best pleasure of fucking a slave's ass chute. Quickly, his master withdrew from his raw channel, and, with a smack on his ass, he was sent back to the steward for a quick douche, insertion of his usual butt plug, and then assignment of his daily chores followed by the mandatory three hours of rigorous exercise regime to assure his splendid physique stayed that way. As he quickly left the room, he felt the familiar stream of his master's cum running out of his distended ass hole and down his inner thigh.

It was almost 11 by now and Adam headed for the entryway where he knew his car would be waiting. Sure enough, the Cadillac was in place with the doctor slave kneeling beside the opened back door with his head bowed.

"The black slave in the trunk?" Adam asked.

"Yes, master," the doctor replied humbly.

"Then take me to the Goldsmith & Barnes slave auction barn. You know the place - it's just a few blocks from here - it's the place I bought you."

"Yes, master," the doctor slave answered as he swiftly rose to his feet as soon as his master had entered the car, closed the back door softly, and raced to the driver's position up front, oblivious to his balls and prick swinging vigorously from side to side as he moved.

Within minutes, the large car pulled up to the auction barn and the doctor raced around to open the door for his master. As soon as the master had alighted, the doctor quickly opened the trunk and helped the castrated black slave out onto his feet and then behind his owner, handing the slave's leash to his master.

"Shall I park the car or wait here for you, master?" the doctor asked.

"Park it and return to the auction hall here, slave. I'll wait for you so make it quick," Adam responded as he grabbed the black slave's neck leash and waited outside the hall.

The doctor luckily found an empty parking space close to the hall and, after securing the car, ran back full speed to his master. Adam took his chauffeur's tit-leash and added it to the leash in his hand attached to the neck of the black slave. Without saying a word, he headed off to a distant corner area of the dealer's pens, the two slaves dutifully heeling in back in him. Soon they entered an aisle with pens variously labeled: "Slaves for Drug Experimentation;" "Slaves for Body Parts;" and "Slaves for Rendering." Both of the young slaves in tow were astonished - they never knew such slaves even existed.

All the pens in this area caged slaves that were old, disfigured, injured, obviously worn-out from overwork, chronically ill, or deranged. The few young ones among them had obviously suffered bodily accidents that made them incapable of manual labor or young rogue slaves that, despite every effort, had reacted to their slave training by going mad and were therefore unpredictable and even dangerous. By this time, their bodies were covered with permanent whip scars and even broken bones in an attempt to beat the "madness" out of them.

"Doctor," Adam said as he jerked on his slave's tit-leash. "Study these slaves carefully. I need to cull some of my stock on the plantations and this is where most of them will end up. Make sure they will be classified right."

"Slaves sold for drug experimentation have to have at least a normally functioning immune system and a reasonably healthy body, but not much else is needed. No one cares about musculature, what they look like, their training to date, their sexual abilities, or even their reasoning. All the drug companies care about is a living subject to test drug reactions. Slaves sold to the drug companies usually don't last very long because they're given diseases and then various drugs are administered to study the effect on the disease. Unfortunately for the slaves, most of the drugs don't work and even more of them have such potent side effects the slaves usually die. Nevertheless, the drug companies pay well for healthy specimens - it's a good use of slaves when you think about it. Otherwise, they'd have to use humans like they used to in our recent history. No one wants to go back to that! We usually sell them stock that can't be worked hard anymore - they're worn out - but their bodies are still functioning OK. It'll be your job to make sure they end up in this classification for ready sale to the drug companies. Make sure you don't include any slaves that are already diseased or really sick or we'll get a bad reputation with the drug companies and they'll stop buying our stock. If even one sick slave gets in this lot, it'll be out of your hide and you'll probably end up here yourself if that's the case."

The doctor shuttered as he realized he had to decide between his life and some of his fellow slaves if he were to survive. All he could say was, "Yes, master," as he more seriously studied the flesh crowded into the pen in front of him. All looked healthy enough but all were obviously worn out, bent over in perpetual fatigue and with a hollow look of despair that seemed to be almost universal in slaves 50 or over. Most were covered in whip scars, numerous brandings, and electrical burns as every effort had been expended to get the last ounce of work out of their bodies. When he had been a practicing physician, he never knew (or really cared) how the many drugs he prescribed were tested. Now that he knew, it made sense that society would utilize slaves for the risky tests, but he never realized that slaves were only utilized after all work potential had been squeezed out of them. He wondered if this constituted the best sample for ascertaining drug effectiveness in humans somewhat fresher like his own patients for the main part. Somehow, he was certain the drug companies wouldn't be asking his advice as a slave, so his thoughts seemed totally irrelevant. As a slave, he would do well to avoid being one of their test subjects, worn-out or not.

"Slaves sold for body parts," Adam continued as he pointed to the slaves crowded together in the next pen, "have to be extremely healthy, usually in their youth or mid years, have great immune systems, and often can be put back to work once the part is removed. Slaves can work the mines without eyes, for example, so slaves destined for the mines are usually put in here first so their owners can sell their retinas for an extra profit. Slaves don't need both kidneys, so often owners, especially those suffering a cash flow problem, often put their slaves in here to sell one of their kidneys. After a month or so, they can be put right back to heavy work with only a tell-tale scar. Now that penile transplants are fashionable, long, thick penises can be sold in that slaves not serving as studs or pleasure slaves don't need them anyway to perform their work. Lung transplants, heart transplants, and liver transplants all require a good healthy donor. Unfortunately the donor doesn't survive the operation so the price is high, often much more than the slave would bring being marketed for his labor or talent alone. A lot of untrained slaves, or slaves not adapting to their training, or mentally retarded slaves, or recalcitrant slaves end up in this pen as long as they're good and healthy and even that refuse brings a mighty good price at auction. Your job, doctor, is to sort out those plantation slaves that would bring more being sold from this pen than they would possibly earn for me back on the plantation. That and, of course, sorting out those that could have parts sold off that wouldn't really interfere with their work assignments at the plantation once they had recovered from the body loss. Not all slaves need to see, or hear, or be able to fuck, to need their hair, both kidneys, both balls, their teeth, or a lot of other valuable parts in order to adequately perform their work duties at the plantation. Your job is to increase our profits considerably by offering those parts up on the open market. Failure to up our profits in this area will only lead to your own sale as a primary organ donor, i.e., those donors that don't survive the operation. So it's strictly in your best interests to do a good job making sure what of my stock can be profitably sold ends up in this pen. Most of the real money is where the donor doesn't return to us, but plenty of money can still be made in offering the hair, ear canals, retinas, skin, penises, balls, and other parts that really aren't needed for continuing to work hard at the plantation once the purchased parts are removed. I hope you understand now, doctor, just why I bought you - it wasn't just to fuck your ass or mouth, delightful as that has proven to be, but any good looking well-equipped slave can satisfy their owners in that department. You were bought to increase my profits considerably. Do you understand, doctor?"

"Yes, master," I answered miserably with tears rolling down my cheeks as I stared into the eyes of the young healthy slaves destined to lose forever certain parts of their bodies if they were lucky and their lives if they weren't quite so lucky. Either way they lost - but losing was a slave's destiny. First their freedom, now their bodies.

"The third pen here contains slaves so sick, damaged, or worn out they essentially have no value left - either in work potential or in body parts. All their bodies are good for now is fertilizer and pet food. They bring very little and are literally sold by the pound, but the little we get on them beats the cost of continuing to feed them. Once a slave can't produce, his life is essentially over and your job, doctor, is to cull these laggards out of the work force and get what we can for them as dog food. There's nothing worse than feeding a slave who can no longer contribute. If I ever catch you letting a slave get to that level before he's for sale in this pen, you'll find yourself punished so hard it would be a relief to be sold off as dog food just to end the pain. Understand, doctor?"

"Yes, master," I state as I uncontrollably broke into sobs. Fortunately, my lack of control was hidden by the loud groans and howls of anguish from those poor penned creatures knowing they soon faced the grinders of the fertilizer and pet food plants. Master Adam rather insouciantly informed me it was customary to feed them into the grinders live in that: (1) their meat tasted better if it was flooded with hormones as the trauma of their death insured; and (2) it cost to put a bullet through their heads first and maximum profit was everything in this business.

Just at that moment, a buyer bought 2000 pounds of slavemeat. Fifteen closely shackled slaves were dragged out and placed on a scale. Due to their emaciated condition, they had to add two more before the scale tipped over the one-ton mark. "Sold to Acme Pet Food," he buyer announced proudly, as the slaves were hustled into a waiting heavily barred slave transport truck for their trip to the rendering plant for a quick, painful, but certain death. Once there, they would be hosed down, have their shackles and slave collars removed along with any tit rings or genitals bands, have their teeth pulled for their ivory, have all hair removed for mattress stuffing, and then unceremoniously be shoved into the churning grinders. It was a typical natural death of a slave, few of whom were lucky enough to die of heart attacks or choke to death with exhausted, worn-out lungs.

The castrated black, only 18, had seen nothing of this side of slavery, and when reality hit home, he could do nothing but retch knowing such an action would only anger his master and likely be the source of new bodily pain. But, luckily, the noise of the wailing, despairing slaves drowned his retching out and he was able to vomit into a pen so it couldn't be distinguished from that of the doomed slaves within. As soon as his stomach was emptied, his only reaction was a frozen look of raw horror and uncontrollable crying which also went unnoticed in the din of the place. The mutilation of his own body seemed as nothing compared to these slaves' plight, although at the time of his castration, loss of his manhood had seemed overwhelming to him. Now, strangely, he was glad he was only castrated. It seemed as nothing compared to having your eyes sold, your heart donated, or being churned into fertilizer while still alive. The fact he was a slave and helpless to change anything that happened to him only made him even more subservient and obedient as raw fear replaced reason.

"Would you like to examine some of the stock here, doctor?" Adam asked rather pointedly. "You'll have to be quick in that I have a noon appointment."

The doctor knew he was expected to examine something, so he selected a handsome young slave, obviously either insane or severely retarded, put up for sale for his organs. The handlers quickly grabbed the selected slave and hauled him out of the cage for the inspection. The slave, terrified, trembled and then peed over himself in raw fear as the doctor ran his hands over the strong, young body. Breathing was ragged, he noted - not unusual for a terrified patient - but strong. Pulse was high but steady, indicating the slave's blood pressure was high as a reaction to what was happening to him. Musculature was well defined and solid. When the doctor reached down to cut the sexual organs, he found them erect and throbbing - not unusual in a healthy man reacting to a terror situation. He reached up and pressed his palm against the racing heart. The slave would make an ideal candidate for donating a heart, lung, or liver. He also had a full head of hair, ready to be transplanted; a good-sized penis that might look good on a new owner, and he obviously could see and hear as noted from his reactions to the examination so his auditory and visual components could be harvested for the right owner. If he were lucky, he could stumble back to whether he came minus only his eyes or his hearing, his penis, or some skin. But most likely, he would be donating a vital organ and could look forward to at least a quick death under anesthesia. After what he'd seen in the rendering sales pen, he almost felt he would be doing the slave a favor to offer him up as a heart donor. With a shudder, he realized such thinking was his salvation for his new assigned task.

Slavery was, simply, the choice between bad alternatives. If you can die painlessly, death becomes attractive. Losing an eye is better than losing your life. Anything beat being worked year after year until you're half-dead and then being ground alive into dog food. As long as he looked at his new assignment in this fashion, he could survive, he rationalized.

Nearby he noticed several slaves whose neck collars and clean loin clothes indicated they were owned by some well-known surgeons familiar to the doctor. They were obviously sent here to pick out "donors" for their master's upcoming transplant surgeries. After checking for blood type compatibility and other factors, they swiftly selected two heart donors (a big muscular blonde and a sturdy negro, both in their early twenties); a lung donor (an Asian slave who seemed to be no more than 19 or so); a cochlea donor (an extremely handsome and well-built teenage Mexican slave, obviously utilized as a pleasure slave by his owner, whose duties wouldn't be impaired by losing half of his hearing ability), and a penis transplant donor (a labor slave extremely ugly and almost grotesquely muscular, but whose penis was at least 10x4 even flaccid). The first three slaves would find a quick death in the transplant; the last two would be returned to their original duties once the operation was over and the wounds had healed. The price of all five was relatively high due to their good health and youth, although the better looking specimens brought the best prices with the ugly work slave bringing less than a fourth of the others. But the latter two would be resold at a good price in that they would still be put to work: the beautiful Mexican boy could suck and be fucked just as well minus a cochlea; the grotesquely muscular work slave could work under the whip just as well with or without a penis. The doctor had always admired the skill necessary for successful transplant operations. He had never really thought much, until now, about where the donors were located. Long ago, he understood they used accident victims who had just died for such purposes. Now, with slaves widely available, the number of available donors had mushroomed, and the surgery was frequently scheduled. The doctors realized a lot of the advances in his own professional field had been made possible by having access to a wide pool of helpless slaves in the society. Such was the price of progress, he thought, and he reminded himself of his many patients who had benefitted from transplant operations over the years. They did important things and contributed to the society in many ways - that wouldn't have been possible without utilizing relatively worthless slaves where they could be effectively medically utilized.

"Seen enough, doctor?" Adam said impatiently as the doctor continued to feel the slave's racing heart.

"Yes, master," the doctor answered, turning, along with the black castrated slave, to heel behind their master once again.

CHAPTER 9

THE TRADE

Adam and his two slaves swiftly returned to the auction barn as it was almost noon. Along the way, the extremely handsome castrated black received a lot of admiring looks and even the doctor, being displayed entirely nude of course, noticed some lustful glances thrown his way.

"If you want to sell the black, let me know," one admirer said as he slapped the black slave on his ass.

"He's headed for a potential buyer right now," Adam said happily, "but you should know he's been castrated. I had his balls packed with steel balls so he looks normal. They did a good job, don't you think?" Adam said as he reached down and hefted the black's balls in his hand.

"Damn good," the onlooker said admiringly. "You'd never know he's been cut. Who are you selling him to if I may ask?"

"Actually, I'm trading him for another slave a woman has. I think she'll give up her slave when she sees this one."

"I don't know what this other slave looks like, but if she beds her slaves down I'd think she'd like a boy that had been nutted for her own protection, especially a boy looking this good. Saves a lot of effort, if you know what I mean."

"That's what I figure," Adam replied as he again continued toward the auction barn.

His master's remarks confirmed what the black had gleaned from previous comments his master had made: he was to be sold to mistress for the purpose of using his body for her pleasure. He smiled in that he would end up fucking for a living just like his two half-brothers that had been sold off a few weeks ago as studs. Although all three of them had certainly been fucked over and over themselves by male masters (and undoubtedly would in the future too), he was happy he would now be put to pleasuring women as well. He had always preferred fucking over being fucked or having to suck someone off, but knew slaves had no choice in the matter. Now, by chance, he would end up, like his brothers, doing what he really preferred anyway, even though he had learned over the years to enjoy pleasuring a male and actually looked forward to such usage, unlike the dread he always felt when he was first introduced to a master's bed. He intended to make the most of the opportunity while it presented itself and vowed to please the new mistress no matter what she wanted him to do. His walk behind his master took on a new spring as his huge organ swelled to full erection in reflecting on his fate. After viewing the contents of the pens they had just visited, he realized how lucky he was that he was born with outstanding good looks, an almost perfect body, and huge sexual equipment which responded quickly and reliably. Those assets alone assured he would be purchased for sexual usage, a relatively easy life compared to that of other slaves. He intended to enjoy this assigned role as long as his body held out. Then, he knew, he'd end up like the others - but that was a long way off.

Within another minute, they arrived at the auction barn and spotted a rather homely middle-aged lady holding the collar leash of a breathtakingly beautiful blonde boy about 20 or so clad only in a super-tight pair of Jockey low-rise briefs which only emphasized his huge equipment straining the fabric. The slave had an almost perfect physique, skin as smooth as any woman's, and striking features highlighted by massive pecs topped by prominent ringed tits, a narrow washboarded waist, a nicely rounded full, but muscular butt, and, of course, the massive equipment lurking under the semi-transparent cotton briefs.

"Alice," Adam said as he approached. "You're right on time."

"You too. I appreciate punctuality," Alice responded pleasantly. "I assume the black slave in tow is the one you had in mind for me?"

"Yes, the other boy is far too old for your purposes, and the black is castrated, so you never have to worry about getting knocked up," Adam answered.

"At my age, I really shouldn't have to worry about getting knocked up anymore, but you never know. Some slave women are being successfully bred well into their late forties, they tell me. But despite the fact he's now just half a man, so to speak, he is, I admit, one hell of a looker. Look, he's eager as a stud bull even now," she giggled. "Is it my charms that turn him on or is he always like that?" she giggled again.

"Your charm, Alice, your charm. Although I admit it doesn't take too much to give the boy a boner," Adam laughed with her. "And once you have him in bed, I suspect he knows how to use it too. At least, he does when I order him to fuck another slave for my amusement. The best thing, Alice, is he never wears out. You know, no debilitating orgasm to take the drive out of a bedbuck. This boy can go all night and never wear out until you wear the skin right off his big pole. He'll outlast you, Alice, I guarantee, no matter how many orgasms you can conjure up in a given bout," Adam laughed.

Alice reached over and hefted the large balls with her small hand and, after 'weighing" the balls, begin to run her hand up and down the whole length of the swollen shaft as she tried to wrap her hand around it, but failed miserably due to its huge circumference.

"You'd know you're being fucked with that in you," Adam commented as Alice continued to stroke the monstrous organ. "I sold both his half-brothers off as studs and they were equipped just like him. Their new owner tells me he's putting them to stud five or six times a day and they love it with a full load each time. The only problem is they're so big some slave women on the small side can't take them."

"If I can handle this slave here," she said pointing to the beautiful blonde standing at her side, "I can handle this black boy. He's not exactly average, you know."

"No, and he takes a fuck well too, Alice. That's why I want him. The only thing is, I haven't tried out his oral service yet."

"Well, we can take care of that right now. Toby, on your knees with your mouth open, the master here wants you to suck him off," Alice commanded briskly.

"Right here? In front of everyone, mistress?" Toby humbly whispered as tears welled in his eyes.

"Of course, slaveboy. A slave like you can't afford false pride," she threatened, "it doesn't become you. Remind me to order a sound thrashing for you when we get home for your unmitigated insolence."

"Yes, mistress," the blonde slave said apologetically as he slid down to his knees before Adam and opened his mouth wide. "Please, master, may I suck you off, master?" he pleaded.

Adam unzipped his pants and stepped forward until his crotch was in the slaveboy's face. Quickly, the slave retracted the master's organ and swallowed it down his throat in a single gulp before suctioning it strongly while his tongue worked over the head and then, swallowing the head deep within his throat, began tonguing the swelling shaft.

"The slave's well trained in his duties, even if he is, as you say, insolent. If we trade, I'll make sure we beat that out of him quickly. Now, why don't you take my black slave over to one of those inspection rooms and have him fuck you? I'm sure you won't be disappointed. When your slave here finishes with me, I think I'll have him fuck my older slave here to study his technique if it's alright with you, Alice," Adam said as he started to pump the boy's face that was orally servicing him, placing his hands in back of the slave's head to draw him ever closer as he did so.

Alice grabbed the black slave's tit leash and promptly left to an inspection room just a few feet away. As Adam felt his own juices rise within him due to the blonde slave's well-trained sucking skills, he heard Alice screaming in delight as she lowered her body onto the black slave prone beneath her and began to ride him at full gallop. As he studied her rhythmic screams and the black slave's accompanying moans of ecstasy, he felt his own juices flooding in surge after surge down the blonde slave's constricting throat, now pumping his shaft with his well-trained throat muscles to extract the last drop of his user's discharge deep into his stomach. When Adam withdrew, exhausted, the slaveboy quickly cleaned his prick of any remaining residue with his tongue and then gently reinserted the organ back into the master's pants opening and zipped it close before again lowering his head in subservience.

"Thank you, master, for letting me suck you. Now do you want me to fuck your slave?" the blonde slave humbly asked.

"Yes. Doctor, on your hands and knees with your knees wide apart to best expose your hole. You're going to get fucked right here in front of everyone," Adam said gleefully.

"Yes, master," the doctor said miserably as he quickly assumed the commanded position, tearing again flowing down his cheeks from the humiliation and shame.

Quickly the young blonde mounted him and thrust his large organ well up his chute. Without hesitation, he began pounding the large tool in and out as the slave beneath him groaned from the assault. The blonde slave shifted positions only once to place his arms around the older slave beneath him in order to work his tits as he fucked him with full force. The doctor responded to the tit play immediately as evidenced by his own swelling organ, now dripping copiously beneath him as he was being fucked. It was evidence to all witnessing the event that the doctor responded well to being fucked and indeed sexually responded to another male taking his ass. Some of the people crowding in around them to witness the public scene commented as much, which only increased the doctor's shame.

"The slave getting fucked sure likes it - look at that boner he's got," one young teenager commented.

"Yeah, and he's dripping to boot. That means he really likes it," another teenager added, no doubt to establish his experience in this area.

"That slave fucking him is a real looker," an older man commented.

"He's that all right, but when you match it with that equipment of his, you can only imagine what something like that would cost you," his son added dryly with a wistful look. "I'm sure I can't afford anything like that, much as I would like to.

"You and me both, son," the father replied. "But that doesn't mean we can't look and dream. He's especially appealing with that blonde hair on his head but how does he get that jet-black pencil-line beard on his jawline. I wonder if they dye that beard to get it that color or if his head hair is died? Fuck the boy harder, slave, fuck him harder," he yelled at the blonde in encouragement who was now covered in sweat and breathing rather hard in his efforts.

"May I shoot, master?" the beautiful blonde-haired slave asked his temporary master.

"No, slave. Your mistress may want to use you right away if we don't trade and I sure as hell will want to use you if we do trade. Just keep pumping away until I tell you to stop, but hold it in, boy, you hear?"

"Yes, master," the boy replied, grimacing as he struggled to contain his impeding eruption into the ass beneath him.

The blonde slave's struggles ended with his mistress' return. His temporary master told him to withdraw and go stand beside his mistress which he did with his prick still rampant and covered with the slime of ass juices while some drops of pre-cum steadily oozed out of the pulsating shaft's hole. The black slave's prick, too, was fully hard and covered with juices and his body too was sweat covered from his recent usage.

"Trade even, like you said, Adam?" Alice indicated she was willing to trade.

"I'm good for my word. Was the black slave satisfactory, Alice?" Adam asked.

"More than satisfactory - divine is a better word," Alice said lustily. "I can hardly wait to bed him down at home."

"And your blonde has a good mouth on him," Adam replied. "He's as good in that area as when I fucked him when we first met."

The two traded leashes and headed for the first notary public they could find to legalize the transfer of ownership.

"We'll need to set a value on the properties," the notary public commented. "I can't just say you traded."

"Put down $600,000 for each one if that's alright with you Alice. That way, when we sell them, it will give the new owner some idea of what a good buy they're getting," Adam said jocularly.

"You're clever, Adam. I like that," Alice agreed. "$600,000 for each it is."

The notary quickly completed the papers, had the sellers and new owners sign appropriately, and then notarized the "sale." The black and the blonde now had new owners and a new life ahead of them.

Before the night was over, the black had fucked his new female owner so many times he had lost count, but the skin on his shaft was rubbed raw and he was utterly exhausted. The blonde had been fucked three times by his new male owner before he was asked to suck his master's Italian slave off so his master could see his throat muscles in action, an act that left his jaw muscles aching from accommodating the Italian slave's huge size. His ass, unused to being fucked, was raw and sore, and when he was finally caged for the night after being thoroughly douched and relubed, he quickly fell into a deep sleep of utter exhaustion, knowing tomorrow probably held more of the same.

Both slaveboys knew they were fortunate enough to be born with attributes that made them the epitome of sexual attraction for both males and females. As such they were valuable commodities and as sexual slaves enjoyed care and benefits not even dreamed about by their less attractive brethren toiling away in the mines, the plantations, the city sanitation departments, and exhausting, fast paced factory work. Therefore, they did everything their owners asked without hesitation and any thoughts of rebellion, even a hint of resistance, never crossed their minds. Their bodies were sold for use by their owners and they knew it. It was their responsibility to make sure their owners were totally and completely satisfied with that use at all times. Both knew that all too soon, those attractive attributes would fade with age and then they would have to face the same realities most other slaves faced - endless toil under a chronic whip and electric prods, starvation feed, sale of their body parts as convenient for their owner, and a certain quick death they minute they were no longer useful for their work potential. Until that time, they intended to take advantage of their beautiful bodies. When they were asked to perform again tomorrow for their owner's pleasure, they would do so willingly, without hesitation, and with an eagerness their owner would appreciate no matter how sore their ass, jaw, or prick felt right now.

CHAPTER 10

THE PLANTATION

The doctor drove his master the three hours it took to get to plantation. Here his master caged over 10,000 slaves, engaged in slave husbandry so the numbers increased daily, and brought huge crops of swine, beef, milk, grain, cotton, vegetables, and tanned leather to market daily. The operation was extremely profitable, despite the huge costs for the slaves providing all the labor, primarily due to its efficient administration by a small coterie of trusted slave-overseers. These "bossmen" saw that everything was done on a given schedule, the slaves were worked to the maximum but not overworked, and that breeding was strictly controlled, not only with the hogs and cattle, but with the slaves as well. On the way out, Adam explained to the doctor that slaves at the plantation were mainly home-bred slaves, being born and raised right where they now worked but that about 20% had been bought in various markets from time to time to add variety to the breeding stock and to meet labor demands as the plantation continued to expand. Those purchased had been relatively cheap in that they were bought for their endurance and strength, not their looks. When any slave could no longer meet a full-day's schedule, he or she was immediately eliminated in that feeding a slave for less than full productivity was stupid, even if some poorly managed plantations still carried on that primitive practice. Therefore, he wouldn't see many slaves over 50 and he certainly wouldn't see any slaves that were crippled, diseased, or sickly. Those, hopefully, had all been shipped to the pens he had shown me a week or so ago at the slave dealers. He added I would see some, though, who had parts missing - like eyes or ears, teeth, or even penises - who had those parts sold off over a period of time for added profit when it didn't interfere with their work responsibilities at the plantation. My job, he stated, would be to identify those healthy slaves who could have some body parts profitably harvested and then returned to work, identify those who should be sent to the rendering plants, and identify those young and exceptionally healthy slaves who could be sold off as major organ donors if the price were right. In addition, if I came across any suffering from disease or recurring illness, I was to get them shuttled into a trip to the dealer for a quick sale to the rendering plants in that the plantation stocked nothing but workable, totally healthy slaves at all times. He added, rather threateningly, that he expected I would find a considerable number in all three categories. Failure to do so would lead to some very memorable punishments and probably sale, after being beat into oblivion, to the rendering plants myself.

"I didn't buy you, doctor, just to fuck your ass, you know. I do have some respect for your profession, even if most of you are arrogant intolerable sons-of-bitches," Adam laughed. "I want to utilize the latest medical knowledge in good slave management," he added, rather proudly. "The plantation has an enviable reputation in that area."

"Yes, master," I responded, dreading, but yet fascinated, at the task ahead of me. Never in my training as a physician had I exercised such power over others - all I could really do was advise my patients - but now my knowledge turned into real power, and the feeling was somehow heady. I felt conflicted: I was sending people to their death; on the other hand I was practicing medicine for the first time since I had been enslaved. It was thrilling but somehow also sickening. Regardless, as a slave, I had to do it.

After kneeling beside my master's opened door upon arrival, he took my leash and led me into the administrative offices: a plain concrete building with no luxuries and staffed by five slave overseers, called to the building to greet their master. My master quickly informed them of my purpose in their operation and how I would be staying with them for at least five or six months until all the stock had been reclassified and processed accordingly. He was to receive weekly reports on my classifications from me, and separate reports from each of the five overseers as to my classifications as a double check, as well as reports on my behavior and compliance to their demands during my stay there. I was to be treated like any other slave, he stated, with no special privileges: the same food, the same sleep periods, the same discipline. The only difference would be that three hours of each day would be spent in a mandatory exercise regime to keep my physique in top shape, that I would need a laptop computer to keep my records, and I was not to be subject to their breeding schedules. They would be responsible for setting up the inspection schedules, getting the slaves to me at a designated place at the assigned time, disciplining me as necessary, and making sure I exercised and stayed in good health. They could use me sexually if they wished just as they had the right to use any slave under them for that purpose, but not to the point where it interfered with my main mission at the plantation: the classification of the slaves. One asked if they too were to be classified by the physician slave whereupon the master answered with a quick yes. This struck a note of fear in each of the overseers; now well beyond their most youthful years.

"But if you even hint at trying to bribe this physician, offering him special favors in return for a favorable classification, I'll personally see you're sent immediately to the rendering plants. Therefore, I expect the physician to be under full discipline at all times, and, doctor, I expect at least one of these overseers to be classified in the "for sale" category. Anything less, and I'll just put you in that category yourself." The overseers blanched at this last announcement, knowing that at least one of them would be sold off as an organ donor or sent to the rendering plants - either way a certain death. "In the meantime, I'll be carefully reviewing your work output records and slave-injury records. Your job is to get maximum output with the least loss of property value - all at the lowest possible cost of maintenance. My review will reveal whose working hard at this goal and who is a slacker." Again, the slave overseers trembled in fear and stared down at their feet as they contemplated their plight.

"You, Overseer A," Adam said harshly to a slave with a huge "A" branded across his upper torso front and back, "what's your breeding productivity ratio. Remember, I expect an overall increase in slave stock of at least 5% a year despite how hard we're working them off."

"Yes, master," Overseer A humbly responded. "My slave battalion is reproducing well enough to reach an 11% ratio this year," he answered as he sunk to his knees and bowed his head, appropriate for a slave reporting to his master.

"Well, you could get that rate by not working the stock hard enough and upping the life span," Adam shot back critically. "What's your death rate?"

"Eight percent, master, even higher than last year," the overseer responded quickly. "I'm working them even harder, master."

"Good, Overseer A, keep up the good work and you yourself could live a little longer," he laughed.

"Thank you, master, thank you," Overseer A responded meekly.

"And you, Overseer B, what's the efficiency rating for your battalion on the cost of upkeep/cost of goods sold ratio?"

"Nine percent, master," the kneeling overseer responded. "Lower than last year, master."

"That's good, Overseer B. The cost of feed and shelter along with first aid costs should never get over 10% of the cost of goods produced or we'd be as inefficient as some of those other plantations not making the big money. Any way you see of getting the maintenance costs down, Overseer B?"

"Yes, master. Do we have to feed them slave chow? Why can't be just feed them garbage we buy from the city municipal departments like the stuff we feed the hogs? If we did that, I'd be able to get my costs down to 4 or 5 percent, master."

"Keep feeding them the chow, Overseer B. It's worth it in the long haul. Although many slaves survive on garbage, I know, they're often not too healthy and they don't hold up under heavy work demands what with vitamin deficiencies, calorie shortages, etc. It's just not worth it in the long haul. When you work slaves hard under the whip, you have to make sure their bodies are well fed, Overseer B, or your death rate is going to climb way up there and you'd be cheating your master out of top profit. In that case, Overseer B, you'd find yourself on the way to the pet food plant yourself."

"Yes master," Overseer B quickly answered. "I'll make sure your stock is fed with the allotted slave chow, master, no matter the costs, now that you've pointed out the advantages to this ignorant slave, master."

"And make sure all five of you eat slave chow yourself. That way you'll stay trim and healthy," Adam added. "Some garbage may look mighty tempting at times, but you stay away from it. You're my property and I want you on slave chow, hear?"

"Yes, master," all five responded together.

"Overseer C, how many whips did you go through last year?"

Overseer C looked petrified, but quickly sputtered out "236 more or less, master, the best I can recall."

"And how many in your battalion?"

"2000, master," Overseer C responded.

"That's less than one a day. A good overseer uses up at least a whip a day if he is maintaining proper motivation. I'm buying quality whips made out of the finest hides and I expect you to use them, not just carry them around thinking you're important. Slaves benefit from a good whipping almost daily - any less and you risk less than maximum output. It's obvious you're getting lazy, Overseer C. I'll have to ask you other overseers to administer at least 5 lashes each to Overseer C until he learns to wear out a whip a day on his stock."

"But master," Overseer C said in absolute panic knowing he probably couldn't survive 20 lashes a day from his colleagues and still function in his job, "I've been using the new Mylar whips you offered us as an option to the leather ones. They last a lot longer. You can look at the backs and rumps of any of my slaves and see I'm keeping them under a very heavy whip all the time."

"I forgot about the new Mylar whips I ordered. They do last considerably longer and bite into the flesh better too. I encourage all of you to switch over to them. A slave beaten with the new Mylar whips knows he's under the whip and the pain lasts longer too. Point well taken, Overseer C, but I can't overlook you spoke out of turn which calls for at least five lashes for impertinence. Overseer A, make sure you use the Mylar for five lashes tonight on Overseer C so he reflects on his impertinence."

"Yes, master, "Overseer A responded. "I'll do it as soon as you're through with us, master."

"Thank you, master, thank you," Overseer C gushed, still dreading the horrible pain he knew five lashes with any whip would give him - a lashing he routinely administered to the slaves under him and had himself routinely received, as the many deep scars on his back and rump would testify, as a common work slave before he was promoted to slave overseer.

"Are you fucking the slaves in your battalion regularly, Overseer D?" Adam asked. "There's nothing like a good fucking to remind slaves they're just bought property."

"Every night I fuck two or three myself, master, but I keep all of my slaves butt plugged every night so their asses are kept open and ready. All of my slaves are able to take a 12 x 4 plug now, master and I make sure it's up their butt all night, master."

"Well done, Overseer D, although plugging a slave is never the same as fucking them."

"No, master," Overseer D responded, fear in his eyes.

"And you, Overseer E, what percent of your battalion has died under your whip this past year?"

"Only three percent, master? Overseer E said nervously.

"Three percent? Is that all, Overseer E? We're not running a nursery school or..." Adam laughed, "a resort here you know. You're probably not working them hard enough. My accountants said five percent is about right. Are you meeting your production goals with such a light hand, Overseer E?" Adam asked.

"Yes, master, 112% last year. It's because I was given such a young crew, master. Most of the slaves are in their 20s yet so they can take a sound beating without dying on you like the old ones in their 40s do. My battalion gets as much of the whip as anyone, master," the slave overseer pleaded.

"Well, they better or you'll find yourself the old man in a young battalion faster than you can spit. How long do you think you'd last in your battalion under a heavy whip these days, Overseer D, spoiled as you are by now?" Adam countered.

The slave overseer turned white. "Not long, master."

"Remember that, Overseer E, when you think of letting up on the whip."

"Now, doctor, I'll have you drive me back to my city abode. After you park the car, we'll have you caged with a lot of new slaves I just purchased and shipped back out here in one of our delivery trucks. When you arrive back here, you can start classifying the stock."

"Yes, master," the doctor answered.

Sure enough, the doctor was right back at the plantation before nightfall. He had been transported in a slave delivery truck along with a batch of newly purchased work slaves. The doctor had never been subject to the usual means of slave transportation: the double decker huge cage trucks with their sturdy mesh floors and closely spaced bars making up the four walls and a ceiling on the top level, and just the barred walls on the lower level. Fortunately, the doctor had been ordered into the top level where at least urine and shit didn't come raining down on your periodically from the slaves above. Nevertheless, it was foul smelling, reeking of sweat, urine, shit, and vomit despite having been hosed down before being loaded. At least 30 others were shoved into each level and, since they had been purchased as just work slaves, they were totally unlike the slaves he had grown accustomed to. Here no one was strikingly handsome, no one had delightfully smooth shaven skin, no one possessed phenomenal sexual organs. Indeed, some were homely, those that were once beautiful had lost their looks to advancing age, most had average sexual equipment if that, some were mutilated or damaged, some had missing body parts, but all were lean and muscular, had unshaven bodies, and most were underfed to the point where their ribs stuck out and they were chronically hungry. Most had backs and rumps covered with whip scars and prod burns and most, but not all, were branded in several different spots, denoting different owners over the years. All but a few had the vacant look of despair and their eyes reflected chronic fear of pain, just a whip lash away.

Most had adjusted to years of slavery by becoming the animals they were treated as. The slaves pissed on each other as the need arose, stooped down to shit when they felt the need no matter who was around them or where they were, and some, sensing that an overseer couldn't see them, prompting began masturbating when the rare opportunity of no supervision appeared. Some were even fucking each other in the press of bodies as more and more slaves were forced into the cage truck by electric prods. All seemed to be a state of constant sexual need and all nervously reacted to any noise that even resembled the snap of a whip or the buzz of an electric prod with a convulsive shudder, a low moan, and terror sweeping into their eyes. Most didn't talk, even to each other, in that years of painful conditioning to respond non-verbally had almost eliminated human speech. They had been bought for the work that could be extracted from their bodies with appropriate discipline and they understood that. Any bodily pleasures would be by accident, oversight, or sneakiness, not by design of their owners. The doctor thought he was in hell and, despite himself, hated the stinking, frantic and fear-driven mass of muscle surrounding him. He could see where people generally despised slaves and referred to them as "animals." These slaves were animals, having lost most human characteristics, such as speech, reflection, spontaneity, and curiosity years ago. With a jolt, he realized such an attitude would help him perform his classification duties much easier.

In an effort to detach himself psychologically from this hell, he began his duties of classification then and there, using the caged animals around him as his first sample. First was a smooth shaved man in his early thirties, obviously once good looking, and still extremely well endowed. Now he looked haggard, his skin was porous and sagging in spots, and his muscles were losing some of their sharp definition. It was obvious he had been a pleasure slave for some man or woman up to his recent sale in that his musculature was the result of gym exercises, not field work, and his sexual organs had obviously been stretched by handling while his asshole could no longer clinch shut. He still was fitted with ringed nipples, a thick genital band, and a high slave collar from his last ownership - all characteristics of a sex slave.

His life now would take a sharp turn. From now on, most sex, other than being used by an overseer now and then, would be but a memory. Muscles would be worked like never before, and he would be working under a constant whip all the time he wasn't sleeping. Within a few weeks, his back and rump, still smooth, would be rippled with permanent whip scars and much of the time his back would be bleeding from fresh whip weals or scalded from the burns of the electric prods. His once beautiful countenance would be mutilated with the brand of the plantation front and back and tit rings, fancy slave collars, and genital bands would all be sold off to some slave dealer fitting out fresh stock for the auctions of new sex slaves. But he was obviously healthy, had many years of work left in his sturdy body, and could be periodically marketed for his body parts not necessary for his work at the plantation: his penis was ideal for a transplant if a color match could be made; at least one eye and one auditory canal would not interfere with his work, and the unscarred skin could be harvested periodically along with his hair follicles. None of these losses would alter his ability to work at all. The doctor could already see him being shipped back to the special pens at Goldsmith & Barnes where body parts were auctioned off, and, once removed by a competent surgeon, then being shipped right back to the battalions of work slaves populating the plantation.

"Did you use to be a sex slave?" he asked the man, now luxuriating by slowly stroking his massive prick.

"Ever since I first entered slavery," the once-handsome man mumbled in response, but didn't slow down in his self-stimulation.

"Was your master a man or woman?" the doctor probed.

"I had many of both over the years. I've been sold 14 times now if my count is right."

"Did you like men or women owners best?" the doctor asked.

"Men owners any time. When they get their rocks off, they leave you alone. With women, there's no end to it," the slave said with little emotion.

"Why were you enslaved?" the doctor asked.

"The usual - my parents had put me up as collateral for a loan and then were forced into bankruptcy. The courts took my brother and sister along with both my parents."

"Were they sex slaves too?" I queried.

"Who knows? I never saw any of them after that first auction, but my brother was good looking and well hung like me at the time. I'm sure my parents were just sold off as labor slaves though - nothing special about them. They could be at this plantation we're going to for all I know," he added without much interest or curiosity.

"I doubt you'll see them there. Most labor slaves don't live much beyond their late forties once they're under the whip. Surely they would be that old now."

"Yeah," was all the slave said, again without a grain of interest as he continued to masturbate himself with ever increasing voracity.

The next slave he studied was totally unshaven, filthy dirty, and was attempting to hump his leg with his swollen organ before the doctor kicked him off. He looked half-starved, appeared to be retarded if it wasn't for the look of chronic raw fear in his very darting wary eyes, and had muscles everywhere. He looked to be in his late twenties, was basically anything but handsome with brutish features, and, despite his large physique, was very poorly sexually endowed. Even hard, as he again tried to hump the doctor's leg, his prick was only 4' long. It was obvious he had been a labor slave for years, especially when you saw the spider web of whip scars crisscrossing his shoulders, back and rump. His rough iron slave collar rubbed the hair off his neck - the only smooth patch of skin on his body. He wouldn't be a candidate for skin transplants due to his hirsuteness, his penis was too small to be salable, his hair follicles might be marketable as would his eyes and auditory organs. Due to his general good health, he would be a good candidate for major organ donation, but only if you could get enough out of him to offset the profits that could be extracted out of at least 20 more years of hard labor before he was completely worn out. He'd recommend him for major organ donation if the price were right.

The slave next to him, in his early twenties, had his lower torso shaved completely, but the huge scar around his lower middle indicated he had just had a kidney removed. Similarly, the slave had recently lost one eye and one ear, and a small, but functional stump between his legs indicated they had harvested his penis while he was on the operating table. Kidney, eye, ear, and penis all in one harvesting, the doctor thought. The profits made off his body must have been considerable and now he was heading right back to the plantation to resume a full work load, none the harm for a few missing parts here and there.

"How long have you been at the plantation?" the doctor asked.

The slave being addressed cocked his head to one side to better hear the person talking to him and squinted through his remaining eye at his inquisitor. "Born there," he answered, leaving it to me to figure out he was a product of their breeding operations.

Fully recovered, it appeared he could be worked for a good 20 or even 30 years more during which time a few more parts could be sold off. Even after all that, there would be enough of him to sell to a rendering plant when his body completely played out and the whips and prods proved futile in getting him to keep up the pace.

Still another slave had obviously gone mad somewhere along the line and had to be kept closely shackled. But properly constrained, and with a steady whip on him, the manual labor required at the plantation really didn't need a brain as long as the slave responded to the whip with solid effort. He seemed incapable of speech until I realized his last owner had torn his tongue out - no doubt tiring of the mad slaves endless screams and constant babbling. He had been fitted with a permanent tight fitting harness which told me he had been used as a draft animal to pull wagons and plows probably. His skin mainly consisted of scars at this point, and the harness had rubbed all the hair off his shoulders and chest when he was hitched up and the harness rubbed against his body in the heavy strain. The long scars on each side of his mouth indicated his last owner also kept him bitted most of the time, suggesting he may have even been used to pull carriages or carts. Looking down, I saw his balls were shriveled and badly burnt. Obviously his last overseer had controlled him with an electric ball shocker as well as the whip, a device that was permanently fastened to the slave's balls and remotely controlled by his overseer. From the badly burnt balls, it was clear the overseer had utilized the device until it was no longer effective - there were practically no balls left to burn at this point. It was little wonder the slave had retreated into madness from a world of unbearable pain. Mad or not, I reflected, he would make a good major organ donator: his lungs, heart and liver would be sturdy and disease resistant and madness affects none of those organs. I felt good about being put into a position where I could end the madman's agony with his bodily contribution to his betters. The doctor pondered whether the slave had been born to this destiny or at some point had experienced life as a freeman. He suspected the latter - it was always harder to accept slavery when you'd once been free. He was a testament to that himself.

The doctor continued categorizing and classifying his cage mates until the lumbering truck finally arrived at the plantation barns and, with a chorus of sheiks and groans as the whips started raining down on them, the new lot of slaves were quickly branded, recollared, and soundly whipped as part of their initial orientation to their new home. The smell of burning flesh permeated the air as one by one the new ownership marks were installed on both their right pectoral and left rump of their writhing bodies as new iron collars, with the plantation's name and usual reward notice engraved in them, were welded around their necks and new identification numbers were tattooed onto both of their upper arms as well as their forehead. Within two hours, they were in the fields working furiously to avoid being singled out again for a severe beating. They were off and running in their new life. The doctor, from the sample of this new lot of just purchased or returning plantation slaves, felt he could reach his quotas for each classification fairly easily as long as he didn't dwell on the fate of individual slaves, but concentrated on the whole of livestock management. Fortunately, since he was to be utilized as a sex slave by his owner when his duties here were finished, he was exempted from the branding and tattoo procedures and was able to retain his current slave collar, genital band, and tit rings.

CHAPTER 11

CLASSIFYING THE STOCK

The doctor was taken to the "inspection station" as the medical facilities were called and looked over the modern laboratory equipment provided there to check blood type and compatibility, semen count and vitality, protein, vitamin and mineral deficiencies, and check for common diseases. The scales, bone scanner, body depilitator, and even an X-Ray, MRI and CAT scan machine were all relatively new and workable. Gone, however, were the other accouterments common to most medical facilities: rubber gloves for anal and oral inspections; paper robes to cover nakedness, and anesthesia equipment. Slaves were expected to have immune systems which could withstand anyone's fingers stuck up their ass or down their throat, nakedness was the norm, and anesthesia was meaningless when pain was considered good and instructive for a slave. After all, most slaves lost consciousness anyway when the pain overwhelmed them so why waste the money. The exam table (actually a tubular frame) was actually quite flexible with restraints for arms, legs, thighs, waist, neck, chest, and forehead all built in along with a mouth gag, butt plug, and a catheter for the penis (so the slave was robbed of his ability to spit, piss, or shit on you). It featured multiple hinges so legs could be spread wide apart, the body strapped to it could be examined on both sides at any angle, and the entire body could be rotated 360 degrees for the physician's convenience. The device allowed for a quick, but thorough examination of the body strapped to it and saved the examiner from constantly bending down to examine his subject, no matter what part of the body was being examined.

Within the first month, he had completed Battalion A's livestock. Of the 2000 in that battalion of labor slaves, 8% would be sold off for rendering in that they were entering that phrase of their live where it costs more to keep them than they were capable of earning in labor; 35% would be offered up for removal of non-fatal body parts with another 11% classified for major organ donations if a good enough price for their body could be obtained; and the remainder would stay right where they were under a heavy whip and sustaining food allotments. Within those remaining in their present status, five exceptionally healthy, young, and sturdy men with huge muscular physiques and equally large sexual organs were recommended for stud duties in the breeding barns as needed with one hour release from scheduled labor for each commanded studding.

Adam carefully reviewed the doctor's first report and was pleased with the number in each classification and the speed with which his physician slave had accomplished the 2000 examinations.

"Well at least this month, we won't be adding you to the crop being harvested, doctor," Adam said to his physician slave. "Besides, I still enjoy fucking you when I get out here to the plantation. The Italian slave is fine, but still lacks your experience. Start by sucking me, boy, and then, when I'm ready, I want you on your back with your legs up over my shoulder. I intend to fuck the hell out of you this afternoon, doctor."

"Yes, master," the doctor said as he crawled over to between his owner's legs and swallowed the master's large organ eagerly. Soon he felt the organ swell and creep down his throat, but just as the doctor willed his throat muscles to contract and 'pump' the shaft, it was abruptly withdrawn. Immediately, the doctor got on his back with his wide spread legs lifted high. As soon as his master had entered his hole, he lowered his legs onto his owner's shoulders and pushed his ass onto the intruding shaft as far as it would go before contracting his well-trained ass muscles around the pulsating invader. The doctor was alarmed that his hole seemed tight and he really had to concentrate to control his ass muscles: not being fucked regularly was taking its toll. Perhaps he could persuade one of the slave overseers to bed him down on a regular basis so he didn't get too much out of practice, but he doubted it. They had to save their strength for fucking the slaves under their supervision - the master thought it necessary to remind slaves of their status. Perhaps he should get some of the work slaves he examined to fuck him periodically. They would jump at the chance to get some sexual relief and a few of the younger ones who were decently hung were actually attractive once you cleaned them up a bit and overlooked their scared hides. Although most of the work slaves hadn't fucked in years and years and were therefore no doubt clumsy in their lovemaking, it would at least keep his hole open and ready and allow him to practice his techniques on a regular basis. He resolved to start looking for possible candidates in tomorrow's examinations when he started in on Battalion B.

The examinations of Battalion B's work slaves proceeded at the same heady pace and even more satisfying results were reported to his owner. Battalion B, being considerably older on the average, offered 11% for the rendering plants; 25% for the partial organ donor market, and 18% for the major organ donation market if satisfactory prices could be obtained. Culling that herd would call for at least 600 fresh slaves over the next year if productivity was to maintained with the lowest possible maintenance costs. Sales of body parts and bodies sold off for major organ donations would constitute a major cash crop for the plantation and at least two-thirds of the new slaves wouldn't cost a penny: the breeding operations were finally playing off now that the first big crops were coming of age.

Again, Adam had his physician slave suck him while he read the monthly review of his medical work. "Good job, doctor," Adam said, putting the report down and stroking the doctor's hair, pressing his slave's open mouth even tighter into his pubic hair. "We'll need a lot of replacement stock to meet your plan, but... but... "Adam fully unloaded deep into his slave's throat......"but we've got"... we've got...we've got plenty of them coming in from the breeding operations," he gasped out as he completed five more ejaculations down his slave's throat."

The doctor couldn't respond in that his mouth was stuffed full, but sort of nodded in agreement as he continued his strong suctioning. Only when his master had withdrawn his shaft and given the slave the opportunity to thoroughly clean it, did the physician slave respond.

"Yes, master. Thank you, master."

"Thanks for what, doctor? Thanks for complimenting you on your classifications or thanks for allowing you to service me?"

"Both, master. Would you care to fuck me in the ass now, master?" the doctor meekly asked.

"Hold your horses, you eager little whore. Give me a chance to recover and that's exactly what I'd do. Suck me to erection again and then get on all fours with your legs spread wide. I feel like splitting you in half this afternoon, slave."

"Yes, master," the doctor said as once again he swallowed the full length of his master's shaft and began massaging it gently with this tongue and throat muscles. It took some time but eventually his master was fully erect and ordered him on his hands and knees. That fucking lasted for over an hour before his master exploded into his bowels. By that time, his asshole was raw and his chute burned from such prolonged usage.

"You still fuck well, doctor," Adam said as he withdrew his sizable shaft from the stretched hole. "But my Italian boy is offering some real competition - he's getting better each day, especially since I have him soundly beaten if he doesn't show improvement each time I fuck him. Makes him a little nervous at times, but he's putting his heart into it now," Adam added with satisfaction. "I may bring him out with me next month so you can see the improvement for yourself. I had you fuck him before, didn't I?" Adam asked.

"Yes, master," the doctor responded humbly as Adam began to play with his tits and then reached down and massaged his balls and erect prick until finally the doctor could contain himself no longer and begged his owner for permission to shoot.

"Oh, very well, doctor. You realize you're no better than a whore, don't you, whining around for relief all the time."

"Yes, master," the doctor gasped as he spilt load after load into his owner's hand.

"Now lick your mess off my hand and lick all that cum off the floor that's dripped down. You still shoot off like a damn bull, doctor. Isn't anyone around here milking you?"

"No, master," the doctor answered as he carefully licked every drop of his steaming cum off his owner's hand and then crawled over and carefully licked the floor clean.

"Well, it keeps you motivated for my visits. We'll keep your output restricted so you're always ready when I want."

"Yes, master," the doctor said as he swallowed the last remnants of his own cum.

The classification of livestock in Battalions C, D, and E proceeded smoothly over the ensuing months with satisfactory results from Adam's viewpoint. Each morning the doctor saw his plan being implemented as huge cage trucks took load after load of work slaves off to Goldsmith & Barnes for sale of their body parts or sale to the fertilizer and pet food companies or sale to drug companies for experimentation, always returning at least one-third full with fresh and younger stock. Each afternoon, he witnessed fresh slaves being transferred from the breeding barns over to the working battalions as able replacements, destined to a life of hard labor under a steady whip. During his tenure at the plantation, three of the overseers themselves had been sold to drug companies and some lucky slave under their tutelage had replaced them, now whipping others instead of being whipped, and now fucking those under them instead of being fucked. Providence had indeed smiled upon them, even temporarily, and the other slaves took note of this rare opportunity to improve their life and modeled their own behavior so no fault could be found with their own productivity and willing attitude. The doctor had located a few slaves that could serve as stud for his eager hole and who were sexually attractive so he no longer worried about suffering in his skills from lack of practice.

Even when being fucked by these work slaves, however, he never once cheated by shooting off no matter how excited the fucking made him. He was afraid his master would find out and sell him off for drug experimentation if he wasn't always fresh and loaded with cum - after all, he had no idea when his owner would appear and demand his services.

After examining over 10,000 stocks, he only ran across five slaves that recognized him from his previous life. They had been patients of his at one time or another, and, like himself, had run afoul of the law for one reason or another leading to their enslavement.

"Still practicing medicine, I see," one of them said, a mere boy of 15 when the doctor had treated him in his clinic for a venereal disease. "Still, you're just a slave, aren't you, doctor?" the man said pleasantly enough.

"Yes, just a slave, but still utilizing some of the skills I picked up in medical school," the doctor replied as he shoved his finger well up the man's asshole to test for piles. "Now I just classify slaves - I don't treat them or anything," the doctor explained. "I don't think they treat slaves here at this plantation."

"Not that I've heard about," the young slave said unemotionally. "If you get sick, they just get rid of you, so I try to keep healthy."

"As we all do," the doctor said laughing. "Beats the alternatives."

"Did you know that we're sold to rendering plants when we're all worn out?" the young slave said with no rancor in his voice. "At least it's relatively quick, I imagine."

"Yeah, it's that alright, but I think the best way to go is to get sold for a major organ transplant. That way, you just die on the operating table and they have to use plenty of anesthesia to keep you from jerking around in the operation. You just go to sleep and never wake up - beats the grinders at the pet food places."

"I'll remember that, doctor. Thanks for the tip. When the time comes, I'll see if I can manipulate my sale in that market. All the other guys seemed to crave the rendering plants because they think the pain from the grinders would only last 10 or 15 seconds before you were gone, but I don't think they understand about the anesthesia part. That's great! Imagine spending the money for anesthesia just on a slave. I know they wouldn't do it if they didn't have to, but, hey, why not take advantage of it? Thanks again, doctor," the young slave said enthusiastically as the doctor's hand began stroking him vigorously for a semen sample, required each year of all slaves potentially useful in the breeding barns. "You know, when I was free, I always thought you were a good doctor, even though you were an arrogant son-of-a bitch," he laughed. "You're a lot nicer now that you're a slave. I suppose being fucked regularly takes some of that arrogance out of you fast - it sure worked with me," he laughed even harder and then tensed up as he shot a huge load into the test tube the doctor was holding at the tip of his throbbing penis to collect the semen sample.

Adam showed up a few days later with his smooth shaved Italian boy on a tit-leash. As soon as the master fucked me thoroughly, I was ordered to fuck the Italian's ass.

"Isn't he better now?" Adam asked.

"Yes, master," I answered as I plummeting in and off of the tight muscular ass of the beautiful slaveboy.

"Now stick it all the way in, hold it there, and let him pump you with his ass muscles," Adam ordered as I readily complied. I almost squealed as the slaveboy contracted and then relaxed his well-trained ass muscles in a steady rhythm, essentially milking me as I remained rammed up his chute.

"Oh, oh, master, I can't hold it, master, oh…" I moaned in absolute ecstasy.

"Go ahead and shoot, doctor. As loaded as your balls indicated when I felt you a few minutes ago, you'll still have several loads left for me."

"Thank you, master," I gasped as wave after wave of hot cum was pumped deep into the Italian boy's ass as he churned his ass muscles unrelentingly.

Before the afternoon was over, the doctor fucked me twice more, the Italian boy got to fuck me as a special treat for his master's amusement, and the Italian boy was ordered to suck me off for his late afternoon snack.

"Your work here is over for now, doctor. You're going home with me," he stated as he snapped a leash to my collar. "Still remember how to drive a car?"

"Yes, master," I responded humbly, now fully drained. I heeled behind my master alongside the Italian leashed by his tit ring until we reached the car whereupon I was unleashed. I sunk to my knees as I opened the back door for my owner and his Italian slaveboy. Once seated, I rushed to the driver's position and quickly familiarized with my master's new car: the latest model Mercedes. Within a couple of hours we were home, but the Italian boy's mouth and ass had seen a lot of action in those two hours and I had to help him back to his cage in my master's house where he could recoup.

"Welcome home, doctor," the steward said, pointing to my cage, freshly cleaned out in preparation for my homecoming.

CHAPTER 12

THE MISTAKE

Cofkuby was back in his cage next to me, apparently back from the many "loans" he had experienced to the master's business associates. He appeared hollow-eyed and had lost considerable weight, making him look scrawny and somewhat older. On the other side of me, the exhausted Italian slaveboy was caged.

"My God, Cofkuby, what's happened to you?" I whispered once the steward had left the room.

"It's been rough, doctor, but I'm sure glad to see you again. I may even need you doctoring me if the master doesn't let up," he sighed. "He's leased me out to a brothel during the day when he's tending to his business affairs. The customers there are fucking me raw, and milking me dry - I end up being fucked 15 or 20 times every day and have to fuck women and men at least six or seven times before I'm sent back to my cage here. They never give me anything to eat and I've got so my cum in my stomach all the time from all the sucking off I have to do, I've lost my appetite by the time I get to my slave chow here. The steward says I've lost 20 pounds since my lease started. Besides that, I think my asschute is infected - it's so sore and swollen I'm pretty sure of it. Some customer tore me up with an oversized dildo one day just for the fun of it and when I tore, I just knew I'd get infected. I bet that's what's happened or it would have cured itself my now. You know, doctor, I'm sure your ass has bled a little now and then when you've been fucked really hard. Any of us sex slaves are used to that - but this was different - I really got torn with that monster they jammed up me. Since then, I've felt sick most of the time, but I still have to go to the brothel every day, of course."

"The master must really be making a bundle off your lease," the doctor said, "but he's losing his investment in the process. I'll volunteer to treat your infection and suggest you get a little sick leave - he may buy into that if I can convince him your value is depreciating rapidly. On the other hand, Cofkuby," the doctor warned, "he may have me soundly whipped for impertinence and work you all the harder - you know the master better than I do."

"Not really, doctor," Cofkuby replied, "I've just been fucked more by him. But I sure appreciate your willingness to say something to the master. I know every time a slave opens their mouth, they usually end up getting beaten within an inch of their life. No wonder they call us the 'silent ones'."

"You'll make it, Cofkuby," the doctor replied encouragingly. "You're young and sturdy yet and that lease to the whorehouse can't last forever."

"What's the plantation like for a slave?" the Italian asked from the cage on the other side. "It looked pretty nice to me - of course, all I've seen of it is the master's quarters when he took me out there to have you fuck me to see if my skills had improved since you last fucked me. Incidentally, I appreciated your claiming I had improved whether it was true or not. Saved me another beating," the Italian slave smiled.

"Believe you me, you're one lucky slave to be in your cage here," the doctor replied. "Work slaves are treated just like draft animals which they are, I suppose. They're fed twice a day, work 14 or 15 hours under the whip each and every day, and are driven so hard their entire bodies are just a mass of permanent whip scars, not counting the endless bleeding weals in their hide they pick up just working a given shift. They do the work animals and machines used to because slaves are now a lot cheaper than either animals or machines: pulling plows with bits in their mouths and harnessed just like a ox; lifting loads like a power scoop; harvesting crops until their hands are bleeding; planting crops on their hands and knees. Their shit is collected for fertilizer, they just piss while they're working; no one ever shaves them or bathes them; and they're never allowed any sex unless they're sent to the breeding barns to fuck a female slave under their direction or if one of the overseers or foremen want to fuck them while they're trying to get a little sleep at night. They're divided into battalions of 2000 slaves that have a slave overseer and about 100 slave foremen for each battalion. Any foreman that doesn't get the maximum work out of the slaves under his charge is simply put back into harness and one of the others is made foremen who is so glad to escape being beaten himself he simply doesn't care how much he beats the hell out of his fellow slaves. Even then, the master sells off your body parts, like teeth, hair follicles, one of your eyes, ear organs or a kidney, and even your penis for transplant if it will make a profit in that you can still work with those things gone once you recover. When you begin to wear out after a decade or so, you're considered for the market in major organ transplants where you die when they take out your heart, your lungs, or your liver. If none of that happens, they keep working you under a heavy whip until you can no longer keep up the pace no matter how hard they beat you, jolt you with the electric prods, or burn you with the branding irons. Some of the older ones are fitted with electric shockers around their balls - after a few months of being fried by those things - your balls are generally just burnt off. The lucky ones die of a heart attack in the fields; the unlucky ones get sent off to the rendering plants where they're ground up alive so that their meat is loaded with their own adrenalin and tastes better when you're turned into dog food. Interested in volunteering, slaveboy?" the doctor asked unemotionally.

The Italian slaveboy stared at the doctor. "I thought I had it rough - being fucked all the time and led around by a tit-ring stark naked in front of everyone showing hard. Now I see what an idiot I've been. I'll never complain again and count my lucky stars every time someone wants to fuck me." He reflected for a while and then added, "No wonder they expect us to thank them every time we service them with our bodies. They really are doing us a favor."

"You better believe it. Fuckboys are pampered pets compared to what I saw at the plantation - that's real slavery, I guess," the doctor responded. "I want to remind you that's what's ahead of all of us once our bodies no longer attract the masters."

There was silence after that and eventually the soft snores of resting house slaves filled the room.

———————

"Master," the doctor said as he knelt at Adam's feet the next morning after being soundly fucked. "May I speak?"

"Make it brief, slave. You know slaves shouldn't ask questions," Adam replied.

"Cofkuby is in the cage next to me, master, and he's sick with an infection. I only mention it in that I don't want you to lose value in your investment, master."

"You're a slave now, doctor, in case you've forgotten. Not the known-it-all asshole you used to be. You'll be soundly beaten for your impertinence in speaking about matters that don't concern you - five lashes minimum tonight."

"Yes, master. Of course, master," the doctor replied. "I could easily treat Cofkuby's infection when he's caged at night with no cost to you, master. It would save his value, master."

"Five more lashes, doctor, for your continuing impertinence. Perhaps some time as a work slave out at the plantation would do you some good," Adam threatened.

"I'm sorry, master. No offense intended, master," the doctor answered humbly.

"Ten lashes tonight for your impertinence, doctor. But I will let you treat Cofkuby when he's penned at night. Tell the steward what you need for the treatment, doctor."

"Thank you, master."

"And, doctor, I'll remind you to never speak out of turn again to your master," Adam added. "Otherwise, perhaps we need to start selling some of your body parts off."

"Yes, master," the doctor responded. "Could I service you with my mouth now, master?" in an effort to get his master off the topic of his slave's insolence.

"Chad, good to see you again," Adam said as Cofkuby ushered his friend into the sitting room. "Some chilled wine? I just opened a bottle of a new Turkish blend."

"No thanks, Adam, but I've got to tell you what I heard down at the slave dealers Goldsmith & Barnes this afternoon," he gushed out as he rubbed his hand over Cofkuby's butt and then hefted the slaveboy's balls in his hand.

"I see you got this boy back up to his proper weight level - he looks as fit and healthy as he used to. That lease wasn't such a swift idea, Adam - those brothels work stock that doesn't belong to them to death - after all, it's no skin off their backs once the lease is signed. Ever since the lease expired and he's been back here full time, he's recovered nicely. I'd say he'd bring in as much up on the block down at Goldsmith & Barnes as he would have before the lease if you marketed him right. Interested?" he asked as he stoked the slaveboy until he was hard and dripping. "Seems like he can still get it up properly," he commented. "His ass tightened back up?"

"Yes. A little rest and the right exercises will do it every time," Adam said. "He fucks just as well as he ever did - at least now I don't notice any difference - I sure did before. But enough about my slaveboy - what did you hear down at the dealers?"

"I'll tell you if you let me fuck Cofkuby," Chad teased. "I haven't had him in over a week now."

"Oh, very well. But first, what did you hear?" Adam pressed.

Chad got serious but didn't let go of Cofkuby's prick. "The police were asking the dealer's recorder who bought your doctor slave. The recorder told me because he knew I was good friends with you, Adam, and thought you ought to know."

"Why are the police interested in a sale made almost three years ago?" Adam asked, obviously puzzled.

"That's what the recorder couldn't figure out. It's seldom, he said, that the police ever want to know who buys anyone committed to slavery by the courts like your doctor slave. What was he committed for, anyway? Drugs, wasn't it?"

"Sort of. He was hooked on cocaine and borrowed to buy the stuff in every increasing quantities. He ran up huge loans and then couldn't pay them off. Fairly routine, really. Life enslavement for indebtedness. Common enough," Adam retorted. "Still, it's curious."

"Sounds routine as an old shoe to me, Adam. Maybe they had him mixed up with some other slave. Now, what about fucking Cofkuby here?"

"Oh, go ahead as long as I can watch," Adam smiled. "How do you want him this time? On his hands and knees or flat on his back?"

"Doggie-style this afternoon, Adam. That way you can see the ends and outs better," he laughed as he whipped off his clothes and promptly entered the slave's ass offered to him readily.

"Yes, officer, I do own the former Dr. Leon Smith. He's renamed "Doctor" now and serves me here in the house. "Bought him at great expense down at Goldsmith & Barnes," Adam answered their inquiry at the front door. "Would you care to come in?"

"If you don't mind. We have a few questions to ask you, with your permission of course."

"Well, I'll answer them if I can, officers," Adam said pleasantly. "I can't imagine why the police would be interested in just a slave - after all, he was sold about 2 or 3 years ago."

"Twenty-nine months and three days ago to be exact for a selling price of $760,000 due to his physician background and startling good looks according to the dealer's records. It also noted he was trained and then sold in the sex-slave department. That's a mighty expensive slave, mister," the policeman said, "even for a good-looking sex slave."

"Yes, he was very expensive, but I still don't understand why you're here? I have a properly notarized certificate of ownership on the boy," Adam responded.

"Well, sir, there's been sort of a scandal down at the court's record office. To make a long story short, it turns out the physician that was sold had paid all his debts on time but they were never recorded due to a clerk embezzling them at the court's offices. The debts amounted to $202, 534 and they were all paid promptly and on schedule - you know yourself how doctors just rake it in these days. The court clerk pocketed the money and reported they had never been paid. The court, of course, committed the doctor for non-payment of debt, a fact established by their own records. Therefore, they never once entertained the appeal from the doctor or his lawyers."

"You mean to tell me it was the court's mistake to enslave him?" Adam asked incredulously.

"Exactly, sir, and they're legally obligated to make it right, respecting your ownership rights, of course. The court is going to ask you to return this particular slave to the court's jurisdiction. They'll reimburse your full purchase price, of course, not even taking out depreciation. They even add, I understand in cases like this, a 10% increment to the original purchase price for his training and another 5% annual increment for feeding and sheltering the slave. That way you should get $950,000 reimbursement for the slave - quite a profit considering you had the use of him all this time," the policeman smiled.

"What if I don't want to sell? Some people tell me that slave's worth at least a million dollars now that he's properly trained."

"Well, that one's a no-brainer, sir. The court will simply issue an injunction for his return and we'll come and get him and you'll get nothing. It's crazy, but that's the way the law is written," the other police chimed in. "The court is going to have its way - one way or the other," he smiled.

"You've made your point, officers. It seems my use of this slave is about to end. What do I have to do to get my money?" Adam asked.

"Just take him down to the main municipal court to Judge Cox - he's the one handling the case. He'll take the slave into custody, make arrangements for repayment of your costs, and you sign the certificate of ownership over to the court. Judge Cox will handle it from there - he's very discrete when it comes to the court's own mistakes and I'm sure he'll find a way to express his gratitude to you for being so cooperative," the first officer replied.

"When?" Adam asked.

"Today, if possible. Is the slave on the premises? We could assist in his transfer if you wished?"

"He's in the forced exercise room right now, I believe. I'll get him unstrapped from the machine and bring him to the foyer here. It'll just take a minute or so, but let me warn you - he'll be all sweaty and probably stink a little."

"We're used to that with slaves, sir," the two policemen laughed.

"You need any clothes on him for the transfer? I have no idea how the court handles their own slaves." Adam asked.

"No clothes. All court slaves are kept naked at all times," the policeman promptly replied as if their answer was self-evident.

"Shall I feed him first, or give him a douche?" Adam pursued the topic.

"Naw - he'll get fed in our own jail tonight and, if he's as good looking as his sales price reflects, he'll get douched out pronto anyway - the jailors always like fucking fresh boys under their custody," both policemen smirked. "If we're lucky, maybe they'll let us the two of us take a crack at him too. It's one of the few fringe benefits we get, sir," they laughed.

Within a minute, the doctor was delivered by his owner to the foyer dripping wet with sweat and leashed by his tit-ring,

"Let's go," Adam said. "I always like to clear my desk fast on matters like this."

The ride down in the squad car to the court building for the four of them (the slave was in the trunk, of course) took only 15 minutes and shortly after that they were in Judge Cox's office who thanked Adam profusely for his cooperative spirit and civil concern. Ownership transfer papers were quickly signed, a requisition for the full reimbursement plus all the bonuses the policemen had indicated was completed and sent to the appropriate office, a form was completed to have the property's slave collar, and all rings and bands installed on the property to be mailed back to him, and the slave itself was escorted to the court's jail for custody. After the policemen had left, Judge Cox handed a check for $25,000 to Adam as a "civic contribution award" given to those who helped the court out in delicate matters and again thanked him for his promptness in dealing with this situation. He promised Adam full cooperation if there was anything his office could do for Adam in the future, ending the deal with a sound handshake and a wink of his eye.

That afternoon, the doctor was indeed fucked soundly and repeatedly by the two policemen before he was turned over to the jailer, who, after feeding him, hosing him down, and douching him thoroughly, had him suck him off and then fucked him three times before the night was over.

CHAPTER 13

MANUMISSION AND AN EX-SLAVES'S DILEMMA

The next morning, he was allowed a warm shower with soap, fed a good breakfast, had his slave collar, his genital band and both his tit rings unceremoniously (but painfully) removed, given some clothes to cover his body (his first clothing in three years), and taken to Judge Cox's office. The judge explained the whole situation, apologized for what had happened, and had the doctor sign the official papers of manumission, legally issued only by a state court. He then handed the doctor $500,000 in cash for lost wages and false enslavement. In return, the doctor had to sign a paper stating he would never discuss the terms of his enslavement or the reason he had been released from the court's original sentence nor would he ever file suit against the state for false enslavement.

Judge Cox then lectured the doctor on the problems of manumitted slaves, a rare commodity indeed in the society. He explained he would have difficulty returning to the life he may have once known: most employers shied away from them; former friends and family tended to avoid them; and he would have difficulty ever regaining social acceptance. He doubted if he could return to his former practice as a physician in that most patients would never go to a doctor that had once been a slave, but he would make sure his medical license was promptly reinstated by court order. Some freed slaves quickly found themselves unable to support themselves in a hostile society and had eventually been reenslaved due to chronic indebtedness. He added that most of those reenslaved adjusted quickly back to their slave status: it was something they understood and they felt accepted. Because of that, they generally brought a fairly high price at auction. He wished the doctor luck in his new life.

"Yes, master," he doctor responded. "Thank you, master,"

"There - see what I mean. You're acting just like a slave and it marks you, boy. Your behavior, altered by the whip over many a year, is a dead giveaway of your previous slave status just as much as that strip of unmanned skin around your neck where your slave collar was. That's why we issued you a turtle-neck shirt - it's to hide that tell-tale white stripe around your neck that will take several months to fade away. You'll find yourself saying "yes, master," and "thank you, master" for a long time yet, as well as automatically kneeling when you're in the presence of someone more powerful than you, like a hospital administrator or something. Even the clothes you're wearing will feel strange and cumbersome for quite some time after being kept nude all the time. I'm sure you're have trouble right now getting used to your sexual organs swinging around freely without a genital cinch holding them in constant protrusion. And, doctor, since I understand you, like most good looking slaves, were used sexually rather extensively by your former owner, you're going to find your sexual interests and needs may have been permanently altered by your years in slavery. You probably prefer sex with men now and probably in the receptive role. I'd advise you to not fight it, but simply accept your new sexual proclivities - the best solution may be to simply buy a slave that would accommodate those interests or rent yourself out to a brothel occasionally. Finally, you've probably had the modesty you once had about your body beaten out of you. You'll have to be careful now that you're free - it would be easy to appear as wanton as a common whore."

"Thank you, master...er...your honor," the doctor responded, rising from his knees and standing humbly before the judge."

"You'll find it difficult to converse like you once did, doctor. Your slave training makes that practically impossible for you now, so your simple direct responses are another giveaway to your slave background," the judge noted. "Good luck and good bye."

"Thank you, master ....er...your honor," the doctor responded, automatically bowing his head.

Just 22 hours before the doctor had been in Adam's sitting room being fucked by his owner as usual. Now, he was a free man, clothed, fed, and rich albeit with a sore ass from last night's fuckings, a sore jaw from all the oral service he had to perform on the jailors, and sore tits from the hasty ring removal. It seemed like a transmogrification if not a miracle.

First, he'd have to rent a nice apartment, buy some decent furniture and appliances, and start looking for a position in his profession. With cash in hand, by noon he had located a nice apartment had a store delivering rooms of furniture and the appropriate appliances by 3 PM. He then decided to visit a small slave dealer located close to his new apartment. While this dealer was nowhere near the size and scope of Goldsmith & Barnes, it specialized in young, handsome boys who were well trained and compliant. He bought a 17-year-old tan-colored muscular Hispanic boy who was exceptionally well hung, good looking, and seemed eager to perform in a new owner's bed. He paid the customary 10% down payment on the boy's $400,000 price and that night used the boy just like he'd been used for the past three years - thoroughly and completely.

When he'd been a slave, he use to dream not of freedom as much as owning a slave himself. His dream had come true, and if his new practice earned him the big bucks he planned, he was going to have a whole stable of handsome slave boys at his disposal just as soon as possible. Adam had been a great teacher in what's important in this life.

But the judge's dire predictions all came true. First, the clinic where he used to practice medicine would have nothing to do with him, claiming no patient would accept medical services from a former slave. Most other similar clinics said, despite his medical license, he was undoubtedly out of date, repeated the unwillingness of patients to patronize an ex-slave, and said other doctors simply wouldn't work with anyone who had once been a slave. The judge had also been right about his social acceptance: none of his former friends would have anything to do with him and he found it practically impossible to establish new relationships once they discovered he had once been enslaved, especially as a slave used sexually by his owner. More than once, he overheard himself referred to as "just a whore" or "he was some guy's fuckboy, you know." As the doctor saw his $500,000 fund decrease alarmingly as rent, food, slave payments, and clothes all had to be paid for, he knew he had to do something drastic if he was to survive as a free man entitled to buy and use slaves.

Reflecting on what he had done well while a slave himself, he quickly honed in on his experience "practicing medicine" in the slave classifications at the plantations. He approached Goldsmith & Barnes about possible employment as a coordinating physician for the organ transplant sales. He could medically assess their own stock for organ parts sales, prepare the stock for the surgeons once they had been selected, and, of those not major organ donors, could sew them back up once their parts had been removed, thereby allowing the skilled surgeons to spend all their time on the purchaser of the slave's part. His simple, but crude, skills in sewing up or cauterizing open wounds would certainly be good enough for slaves being returned as work slaves (nobody cared how such slaves looked as long as they functioned OK) and he was used to the stench of the slave's unwashed, beaten bodies, their frantic looks of utter despair, and their mindless howls of anguish when responding to the overwhelming pain of unanesthetized surgery and the knowledge their body was being sold off piece by piece for their owner's profit. Goldsmith & Barnes quickly saw the advantages of his proposal if the surgeons actually doing the transplants would approve.

They did in that it saved them the part they hated the worst - dealing with screaming, stinking slaves who needed to be sewn back together (if they weren't a major organ dealer). Goldsmith & Barnes thought they would benefit from lower mortality of valuable stock if a trained physician was tending the slaves and knew only a former slave would be able to tolerate the stench from the sweat, piss, vomit and shit emitting from slaves having parts of their body removed. They offered him $100,000 a year - a pittance compared to the salary of a regular physician and approximately a third of what he had once made in private practice. Furthermore, he would have to be on-call around the clock, more or less, in that his work load would depend entirely on organ sales on any particular day. He was expected to classify incoming stock anytime he wasn't busy sewing slaves up so he knew he would probably have to work 70 to 80 hours a week. The price offered was an insult to any self-respecting physician but so what, he thought. Without friends or social acceptance, what else did he have to do with the stigma of being an ex-slave constantly accompanying him? He signed the contract before they changed their minds.

His work at Goldsmith & Barnes worked out fine. He quickly got into the swing of things, increased the efficiency of the organ sales, and his classification of incoming stock proved extremely helpful to the auctioneers working for Goldsmith & Barnes. With his new source of income, he could easily afford a couple of more slaves as long as he bought them on the installment plan and, being right at the biggest dealer in town, he could pick and choose the best.

That's exactly what he did. He first bought a 20-year-old Italian who had served two previous owners already as a sex slave: a master and then a mistress. He was a bred slave and gave his owners no problems whatsoever, no matter what he was ordered to do. The doctor was enamored by the slave's muscular build, his beautiful complexion, his handsome face, and his thick, long organ. He made a nice addition to his stable, consisting up to this point of the lone Hispanic who had proven to be a good investment. A year later, he again added to this stock: this time a huge 25-year-old black that epitomized mature masculine beauty and who sported prodigious sexual equipment. The doctor by this time was bored of always fucking his stock; he enjoyed being fucked by his slaves also and the black was perfect for this task, proving to be forceful but gentle and always totally under his control. The black slave had been enslaved when he was 21 for rape - it was ironic he was now fucking for his keep. With a stable of three at his beck and call, the doctor was content. Between this work, which he enjoyed, and using his stable in his off-hours, he felt fulfilled.

The judge had given him good advice. He avoided the dilemma experienced by many ex-slaves - chronic unemployment, mounting debts, and inability to adapt to a free man's live. Although his life was in no way what it was like before he was enslaved, it didn't bother him. As far as he was concerned, his life was even better. He thanked Adam for that. Adam had shown him what was important and not important in this society and how to benefit from the largess of the social system in place. Adam showed him that slaves were available to be enjoyed and bring their owners pleasure as well as do all the undesirable work. Adam had introduced him, albeit without choice, to a whole new avenue of sexual pleasures to be experienced. Yes, Adam was to be thanked as a great master. He only hoped he was as good a master to his own slaves. Little did he know what would develop next.

CHAPTER 14

A NEW JOB

"Dr. Smith? Dr. Leon Smith?" the smartly dressed middle-aged man inquired as he looked intensely at me.

"Yes, sir," I answered, looking up from the paperwork I was completing on today's slave classifications for my employer, Goldsmith & Barnes, Specialists in Slave Livestock. "Could I help you?"

"Dr. Smith, I'm David Houseman. I'm a business facilitator representing a consortium of surgeons and pharmaceutical company physicians that you have worked with here at Goldsmith & Barnes. My constituents have seen first-hand the high quality of your work here in selecting the best slaves as organ donors as well as subjects for drug experimentation."

"Yes?" I replied cautiously, curious as to where this was going.

"Well, my constituents admire your skill in this crucial area, doctor, but, to cut to the chase, well…. they feel your talent and skill may not be properly appreciated by your current employer," the man said smoothly without embarrassment.

"So?" I slowly prodded with an arched eyebrow.

"Well, doctor," he paused, "they wondered if you might be interested in setting up a slave dealership specializing in donor and drug experimentation slaves that would deal directly and exclusively with a consortium they're setting up. Such an exclusive dealership would effectively cut out the middleman, Goldsmith & Barnes and a few other large dealers, in this lucrative area, doctor, and could prove to be very profitable. Especially," he added meaningfully, "if you were a senior partner in such a consortium."

"Yes, such an enterprise could prove to be extremely profitable," I replied, "but capitalization costs would be extremely high, especially in the startup phases. To properly finance such an exclusive dealership could run as high as 100 million to build the facilities needed, staff it properly, and stock it sufficiently to meet the consortium's needs."

"It's exactly that quick thinking and expertise that impresses the consortium," the smiling man replied. "It's obvious why they wanted me to approach you about such a proposition."

"That's flattering, but doesn't solve the problem of capitalization," I ventured.

"Right to the point, Dr. Smith. I love dealing with you," Mr. Houseman enthused. "Capitalization won't be a problem, even if it runs over the 100 million you cited. Frankly, we thought it would run more like 120 million to start up, but if you can do it for less, more power to you. My constituents are fully prepared to provide the venture capital necessary to get started and have such funds already in escrow for your use. They're not too worried about getting it back - they predict a return of 18 to 22% a year on their investment."

"At least," I added. "I would predict closer to 30% if the place were properly run."

"That's exactly what they said you'd say," the facilitator beamed. "You're obviously the man for the job."

"And what's in it for me?" I asked. "You sort of slid over that!"

"Those putting up the capital would hold 90% of the stock - you'd get the remaining 10% of this wholly owned private corporation that would own the specialized dealership. All profits would be split according to the number of shares each person held, but, Dr. Smith, you'd hold 10% of all the stock yourself. Best of all, you'll be selling to the very firms my constituents work for who have inside information on upcoming needs and specifications. In some respects, it's a no-lose situation or my constituents wouldn't be interested."

"Have they checked out the ethics of this? After all, they're physicians just like myself," I asked.

"You mean about the inside information? They feel they're doing their companies a favor by getting them to buy the best stock available for their purposes. If you're talking about using slaves for these purposes, well...," he laughed, "that issue was settled years ago when slaves were substituted for humans in this area... a huge step forward for society in everyone's opinion. Surely, doctor, you don't have any ethical qualms about what you're doing now for Goldsmith & Barnes?

"Not really," the doctor admitted. "Not when you study the alternatives."

"Well, I would think not," the facilitator shot back. "Did I add they would guarantee you $300,000 base a year if your share of the profits didn't reach that level?"

"They have thought this out better than I reckoned," I replied. "Mr. Houseman, everyone involved realizes I'm a manumitted slave myself, don't they? I don't want to hold anything back."

Mr. Houseman looked uncomfortable and I saw his eyes focus on my neck as if he could envision a thick slave collar still around it.

"My constituents," he replied carefully, still looking very uncomfortable, "speculate that your skill in selecting the best slaves for their purposes at the best possible prices is due to the fact you spent some time in slavery yourself." His eyes shifted to the floor revealing he wished I hadn't brought up the sensitive topic.

"I was a sex slave for almost three years, Mr. Houseman," I deliberately exploited his discomfort. "Fucked repeatedly every day and did about everything else free men and women can dream up for slaves to bring them pleasure. Don't tell me you haven't used a slave or two in your own bed off and on?"

"My personal life isn't at issue here, Dr. Smith," the facilitator sputtered, blushing bright red. "To answer your question, yes, my constituents are well aware of your peculiar background for a freeman, Dr. Smith, and it doesn't bother them in this undertaking. To the contrary, they feel it is an advantage. On the other hand, since we're being totally frank here, they hired me to negotiate with you in that they don't like to associate with an ex-slave - a feeling I'm sure you're used to by this time, and they probably won't associate with you in the future outside of this 'silent partner' business relationship. And, Dr. Smith, since you felt no qualms in trying to embarrass me with your impertinent question, let me answer you directly. I own two sex-slaves myself: a handsome young man extremely well-trained and a beautiful woman with a body like Athena. Most people of my wealth and station have such slaves readily at hand, as you, Dr. Smith, of all people, must realize."

"I apologize for my rudeness, Mr. Houseman," I replied softly. "I was just making sure everyone knew of my past and wasn't bothered by it. It was offensive of me to embarrass you personally like that. I'm sorry."

"Apologies accepted, Dr. Smith. I suppose a person gets a little coarse after what you've been through. Do we have a deal or not?"

"We're on," I promptly replied. "A minimum of 100 million venture capital up front at my disposal with 10% of the shares in the new corporation and a $300,000 base salary guaranteed."

"Exactly. I'll have our lawyer draw up all the papers for your signature while you give Goldsmith & Barnes sufficient notice of terminating your contract with them. There's no need, of course, for them to know at the present time what your future plans are."

"Of course not, Mr. Houseman. Can be shake on it?"

Mr. Houseman quickly thrust his hand forward and firmly shook hands. "I'll have the final papers delivered to you in a day or two. When you've had a chance for your own lawyer to look them over, give me a call and we'll arrange for the final signing. Here's my card."

———————————

After selecting three more slaves as candidates for major organ donations, I left early from work at Goldsmith & Barnes right after lunch with plans to give them my written resignation tomorrow effective in one month. That would give them time to hire a replacement for me and give me time to establish the new dealership. I realized it would take a lot of work on my part to guarantee an adequate and continuing source of new slaves - the best place to start was with the big plantations, construction firms, and factories who were continually culling their stock for more productive replacements and the breeding farms who were steadily increasing their output each and every month. Once I convinced them to give me first choice of their excess stock, I was sure I wouldn't have to worry about stocking the new dealership. My contacts with their sales agents through Goldsmith & Barnes would be of great help - I was familiar and they knew me personally; they knew I could handle the paperwork easily enough; they knew my classification skills brought top price for their stock; and, hopefully, they felt I was a person they could trust to not cheat them.

Without delay, I personally visited the sales agents of the 12 largest sellers of slaves to Goldsmith & Barnes that I had dealt with in the drug experimentation, body parts donors, and rendering plant markets. I explained setting up the new independent specialty parts dealership which would offer top prices, free classification services, and cash on delivery. Although Goldsmith & Barnes generally offered good prices for stock, they took some of that away on each sale by charging for my classification services and paying only after the purchased stock had been resold to the surgeons, drug companies, or rendering places - a process sometimes consuming up to four to five weeks. It was an offer they couldn't refuse and we shook hands on it in every single case. I breathed a sigh of relief! At least, those 12 agents alone could fill my inspection pens for a while.

Next, I needed dealership facilities. I had no idea of where to start on this one since most of my experience had been with the one dealer I worked for - Goldsmith & Barnes and they surely weren't going to provide this new competition any favors! The facility didn't need to be too big - after all this was a specialty market, but, considering the numbers often headed to the rendering plants, there would need to be plenty of holding cages as well as numerous inspection cages and pre-auction preparation cells for the body parts donor and drug experimentation markets. The only dealer I had really visited, outside of my employer Goldsmith & Barnes, was the dealership specializing in sex slaves where I had bought my Hispanic boy several years ago, later the Italian beauty, and, still later, the older black stud. Although their facilities would be just about right for my operation, I saw no reason why that dealer would give up his profitable business in sex slaves to sell the facility to me. Nevertheless, to familiarize myself with what a smaller dealership's facilities were actually like, I decided to visit that specialty dealer again. Who knows, I might even find a new slave that would interest me, especially now that I could easily afford one or two more if I so desired. Owning a "stable" of sex slaves was one luxury I really enjoyed and which my own ex-slave status didn't impede in any way. In a sense, having a "stable" was a substitute for my limited social life as an ex-slave.

Currently, I still had the lusty Hispanic, now 20 years old, who continued to be most satisfying. His ardor in bringing me the utmost pleasure had not abated since I had first purchased him. The handsome Italian boy also had not been sold and never once had failed to do anything I asked of him with enthusiasm and spirit. I particularly enjoyed fucking him face-to-face where I could play with his prominent tits, feel his giant prick pressed between our bodies, and study his beautiful face as I pumped into him deeply, but leisurely, to forestall a rapid eruption on my part. The huge black stud, now 28 and beginning to show some signs of wear and tear, was utilized mainly for fucking me at my pleasure as well as the Hispanic and the Italian when I needed some entertainment. He too was totally satisfactory, never failing to arouse his massive equipment when ordered and seldom failing in his ability to hold off a debilitating emission until especially allowed by his master to do so, a privilege he seldom received. I had decided several weeks ago to sell the black off before he really depreciated on the open market, and replace him with one of the studs periodically sold off by Wilson's Stud Farm, still popular and profitable some 22 miles out of town. I remembered Adam's glowing account of the astonishing pieces of man flesh available there and how the steward had told him about selling some of the stock off as their semen counts started to decline. I figured I could get a real beauty at a bargain price. The stud slave would be well used for sure, but very experienced and well trained. Who knows, maybe I could buy one of those black half-brothers Adam sold him a few years ago. I knew they were good - they had fucked me and visa versa while we were all part of Adam's harem.

But selling off his black and buying a replacement didn't really add to my stable. For that, I was thinking of the relatively rare red heads that occasionally come up for sale, a short, but muscular Greek boy that I always found appealing, or even some exotic - like an Asian or an Arab or a Polynesian boy. Perhaps the sex slave dealership I wanted to visit anyway would stock something like that which would interest me. That way, my trip wouldn't be just to check out their facilities - I would be a genuine customer as well.

When I arrived, the old dealer, well into his 70s judging from his appearance, instantly recognized me from my previous purchases. When I rather blatantly asked if I could view all of his facilities (claiming I was so pleased with my previous purchases I wanted to see how they had been kept at the dealers to prove so satisfactory), he readily agreed. He commented that few customers ever seemed very interested in all a dealer had to provide to maintain and trade good stock and he didn't have anything else to do right at that moment anyway - I had visited at a good time, he stated with a twinkle in his eye. He personally showed me all the holding cages, the preparation cells, the training rooms, the punishment rooms, the bathing and shaving rooms, the enema facilities, the oiling rooms, the exercise rooms, the bodily accouterments fitting room, the inspection cages, the auction room with display stands, and even the business offices located over the main sales areas. The facility was in good shape and had been well maintained. All of the equipment necessary for controlling and training a moderate number of slaves seemed to be on hand. What was notably lacking, however, was available stock.

"Where's all your stock?" I asked. "It seems mighty sparse compared to the last few times I've been here. Did you have a big rush and are just temporarily short stocked or are sex slaves hard to come by these days?"

"Neither," he smiled, "but I can give you an exceptionally good buy on any of the stock that's still around."

I looked quizzical.

"I'm going out of business," the old man smiled. "I'm 75 next month and I promised my wife I'd retire when I hit 75. So I'm having a 'close-out' sale on my stock. You won't find any better bargains anywhere."

"Have you sold your facilities?" I ventured feeling the excitement rise within me. It was obvious, after the inspection tour, that this dealership was exactly the right size and had all the facilities needed for my new enterprise.

"Not yet. I've been scared some buyer would want it right away and then what would I do with this stock?"

"How much are you asking?" I gushed out, revealing my excitement.

"For the stock that's left or the dealership?" the old man shot back.

"The dealership," I quickly interjected.

"Was thinking of asking $260,000 minimum. I know it's old but I've kept it up well - nothing fancy or anything, other than the sales room - but it's really all you need to manage a decent dealership and there's lot of space. A person could even expand the operation considerably if they wanted - there's the space to do it. Of course, the location isn't ideal, I know, but in the speciality markets the buyers more or less find you rather than the other way around."

"How about $280,000 cash and you never even put it on the open market," I looked him straight in the eye. "I can have the money in your hands within a week or so, and I'll give you plenty of time to clear out your remaining stock - say three weeks. If there's not much stock left, I'll even take them on as a retainer - your keep their titles of ownership and I'll peddle them as a third party until all your stock is depleted with just a minimum per diem charge for feeding and housing them."

"You going into slave dealing?" he asked, obviously surprised. "Or are you in the business already?"

"Both, actually. I've been working over at Goldsmith & Barnes for the past three years in charge of drug experimentation, body parts donor, and rendering plant sales. I'm a licensed doctor, you see, and classify slaves for potential sales in those departments. But I've decided to go into business with a consortium of surgeons and drug companies who are sponsoring me to open a new dealership specializing in fulfilling their ever-present needs plus dealing in spent slaves for the rendering plants and pet food companies. We figure it will be most profitable - we plan to cut out the middleman profits and utilize my skill in classifying slaves most effectively for those markets. All we really need now is a decent facility for such an undertaking - this is it," I exclaimed.

The old man paused, stared at me a while and ruminated. Finally, he said, "Well, your offer saves me a whole lot of time and trouble and these bones are getting damn tired, let me tell you. Besides, I run the risk of not even getting my minimum if I put it up for auction. If I list it with a realtor, I've got the 6% fee there and final sale could drag on for years. You've got yourself a deal, Dr...?"

"Dr. Leon Smith, sir," I replied. "I'll have the money within a week. When I get the cash in hand, I'll call you. In the meantime, have your attorney draw up the necessary title transfers and we can get this matter concluded in short order."

"You are fast," the old man smiled extending his hand for the customary hand shake to seal the deal. "$280,000 cash and it's all yours."

"Well, now that that's taken care of, maybe I can concentrate on getting rid of the stock still left around here. If you're interested in any more sex slaves, Dr. Smith, I can sell them to you at rock bottom prices."

A Boner Book

CHAPTER 15

MOVING UP

"Let me look them over," I smiled back. "I was so busy looking at your facilities before I never actually noticed what you had in the cages."

"Look all you want. If you see anything that interests you, we'll haul them out for a thorough inspection," he offered as he led me first to his display stands.

He had five slaves up for display, each chained to their podiums with their hands shackled in back of them. All were totally nude and had been completely body shaved except for their head hair.

"I know you prefer males, so look these over first. I've got some females back in the holding cages if you're interested."

The first was an Asian who was at least 30 and had some permanent whip scars marring his back and rump; the second was a white boy no more than 15 who was emaciated and looked sick with his gray complexion; the third was a well-built Irish boy with flashing blue eyes and black hair, a handsome face, but, unfortunately, was well-below average in genital size.

"You're going to have trouble selling this one," I commented as I reached out and squeezed the boy's small organs. "Not too many want a sex slave equipped like this one," I laughed as the boy under inspection blushed in embarrassment.

"You're right, but some don't mind if the price is right, especially if all they plan to do is fuck him or have him suck them off anyway," the old man said professionally. "But I admit, he's not prime goods," he added, as the slave blushed an even deeper shade of red and looked down at his feet.

The fourth slave was another Asian no more than 5' feet tall and weighing less than 80 pounds. He looked like a toy compared to the others displayed. But he too was not well-equipped and he too looked seriously undernourished with prominent ribs and hip bones marring any attractiveness he may once have had. The fifth slave was very well built, but was pushing 40 if a day and had rather coarse skin as older men tend to get. Despite the fact he was also well-equipped, his years of service were obviously limited.

"Looks like you're down to the bottom of the barrel," I commented. "Other than the Irish boy with the small dick, these slaves are probably best suited for the markets I'm going to be dealing with: body parts donors and rendering plant material. That young white boy is too sick to sell off to the drug companies or to the surgeons - he's strictly pet food at this point. There's not much here that you could sell as a sex slave." The slaves being discussed openly trembled in raw fear as they absorbed the doctor's comments.

"You'd be surprised what sells if the price is right. I know they won't bring much, but some poor bloke would rather have these pathetic creatures to fuck than beating themselves off every night. You can often sell stock off like this to the really poor people who can't afford much else. You get a decent house servant that you can fuck if you don't care what you're sticking it to," the old man counseled. "I'll get them sold - don't worry. The only problem is, they don't last long when you sell them to the down and out - they don't have the money to feed them properly and so they tend to die fast on them. That's why I sell them with no guarantees to that type of buyer."

"Well, I see you know all aspects of your business, but my offer still stands. If you can't get rid of them - I'll buy them by the pound for resale to one of my clients. What's left back in the holding pens?"

"Not much, as you probably have already surmised. But I got a few new ones back there - bought them from one of my competitors that had to declare bankruptcy. Haven't had time to get them ready for display yet."

With that as a warning, the old dealer led me back to the only holding pen actually containing stock. There were less than 10 altogether, 5 of them the new male stock picked up from the competitor. It was obvious the five that weren't new, three males and two females who were even worse than those out on display. The other five, though, were still young and healthy looking. "Could I see those five new slaves you picked up?" I asked.

"Sure," the old man said as he grabbed a whip and ordered the five boys out in the hall where I could look them over.

"Position," the dealer ordered with a crack of his whip and all five boys spread their legs, placed their hands in back of their heads and thrust their pelvises forward for the inspection.

All of them were obviously selected and trained to be sex slaves. They were, to a man, good looking, well built, well-equipped, and, judging from the way they eagerly displayed themselves so wantonly, eager to be sold. As I examined each one in intimate detail, each pleaded with their eyes to be bought, even whispering "Buy me, master," as I fondled them to erection and inserted my fingers up their ass chutes to check for tightness. It was obvious they were desperate to be sold; anything was better than being held in a holding pen day after day enduring endless inspections by potential buyers. Any one of them had 100 times the marketability of those pathetic creatures displayed up front. One was a young mulatto of no more than 17; another was an 18-year-old blonde haired German with extraordinary equipment; another was a 21-year-old Spanish kid with olive skin and jet black hair; another was a 22-year-old Macedonian who was a bred slave; and the fifth was just what I had been looking for: a bright red-haired boy of 19 with smooth creamy skin, an extremely muscular physique, and phenomenal equipment that sprang into full erection the minute I first kneaded his prominent ringed nipples.

"How much for this lot of five?" I asked, trying to hide my excitement over this treasure trove. "If you give me a good enough price, you'll only have 10 left to get rid of," I noted.

"What would you do with five more sex slaves?" he laughed. "I thought you had three at home now," he chuckled. "A man can only do so much, you know," he joked.

"I like having a whole stable of slaves to choose from," I replied. "It's one advantage of being relatively rich, I suppose," I added.

"These five are prime stock, I suppose you realize. But I can give them to you at cost, just to get rid of them, and remember, my cost was damn low - I picked them up at a bankruptcy sale."

"How much?" I repeated.

"For you, the new owner of this dealership, I'll let you have them, as I said, for just what I paid for them yesterday. Still have the bill of sale to prove what I paid for them. $860,000 for all five. They're mortgaged by the banks already, so you only have to pay five percent down and installments over a five year period. $44,000 and you can walk home with all five on a leash," he commented. "That is, if you want to take on a mortgage like that."

"Could I see their provenance?" I asked.

"Of course, Doctor Smith. It's right here attached to the bars of the cage. Keeps it nice and handy," he said as he unclipped the small booklet from the bars briefly outlining each slave's origins and history. The dealer I got them from threw it in with the sale."

I glanced through the one-paragraph outlines on each of the five slaves. They were interesting, but not in any way unusual for sex slaves.

The mulatto had been enslaved at 15 for auto theft, had spent a full year in intensive training, and had experienced two owners since he was released for sale at 16: first a mistress and then a master. His last owner had named him "Sucker" for his outstanding sucking and rimming abilities, noting his tongue was both unusually long and rather course as well as being extremely well trained. The slave was proud of his body and enjoyed being displayed in public. Neither of the previous owners experienced any difficulties whatsoever with him.

The German was an orphan at 14 and consequently had been enslaved by the courts as a minor, long after he had gained considerable sexual experience with one girlfriend after another. He had only completed his sex slave training after he reached full maturity when he was 18, however, and had strongly resisted being used by other males, resenting it, but knowing there was absolutely nothing he could do but cooperate to the fullest as a slave, in being used by male owners since that time. Ironically, his deep resentment turned out to be his major appeal, and both of his owners to date had been males, enjoying having the power to use the male any way they wanted knowing he could do nothing about it despite his shame and embarrassment at being so used. He had been trained to be completely versatile, of course, so the slave had seemingly learned to just grin and bear it while making sure he pleased whoever had bought him. His previous owners particularly enjoyed fucking his tight ass and having him service them orally, the report read. It added he no doubt would prefer a female owner, but the resentment factor did undoubtedly add to his appeal to male owners.

The Macedonian, being a bred slave selectively bred just for this market, had been trained from birth for just what he was doing now. He was cooperative, even eager, in performing his duties for two previous female owners as well as a previous male owner. Due to his extended training period, his sexual skills were unsurpassed.

The Spaniard, enslaved at 18 for drug dealing, was listed as basically heterosexual, but was now perfectly amenable to homosexual duties as commanded since his training in such skills had gone well and resulted in a totally versatile male slave who had pleased each of his four owners to date, both male and female. Due to his natural proclivities, it was suggested future buyers might want to rent him out for studding duties occasionally or even consider selling him off to a stud farm when they were bored with him.

Finally, the red-head, another bred slave, had good reports from the one female owner he'd had since first being put on the auction block. He had been fully trained to service both females and males, of course, so his versatility to future owners was assured.

His previous owner had indeed put this to the test in that he had frequently been loaned out to her men friends as well as service her and all users reported him totally satisfactory, even eager to please them. His phenomenal equipment indicated the boy should be bred when possible for additional profits, something his previous owner had done on occasion with successful impregnation rates.

I put the booklet down and looked at the slaves again, still standing in the commanded "position" stance and all dripping pre-cum in their excitement of being examined. I decided to buy the lot of them.

"It's going to take most of my savings, but I can write you a check for the $44,000 right now and I'm willing to sign the mortgage papers today to seal the deal."

"Sold," the old man practically shouted. "If I can't get rid of the garbage remaining when you come back to close the deal, I'll sell them for the rendering plants by the pound. I'm ready to get rid of the stinking animals and get on with my retirement."

As I wrote the check, the old man found the appropriate ownership titles and signed them over to me. The slaves just sold, still standing in their commanded "position" stance, looked relieved, even the German who realized servicing a man in all ways possible was far better than staying in the holding pens and risking sale as a work slave. Now that he was essentially a whore as a sex slave, the German slave opined, it really didn't matter whether his body was used by males or females - as a slave, it was completely out of his control anyway. Like all sex slaves, he realized his life was very cushy compared to most slaves auctioned off.

"Bring these papers back when we close the deal on the dealership and we'll get them properly notarized so there's no questions asked. Meanwhile, I'll give you a receipt for the $44,000 with each slave listed for your protection in case I drop dead or a car runs over me," he laughed. "I'll see if I can round up five leashes for you to get this meat home. You want any clothes on them for the trip home, or are they all right just as they are?"

"They're fine as they are," I laughed. "No use them getting any clothes - they'll never be allowed to wear them where they're going, anyway, and everyone is used, nowadays, to seeing slaves naked on the streets."

"Yeah, it's seldom you see otherwise anymore," the old man said. "Wasn't that way fifty years ago - people were so prudish and uptight then," he mused. "Slaves were never let out of the house without some rag or another tied around their genitals. Seems silly now, doesn't it?"

Once leashed, the five slaves heeled behind me for the walk back to my apartment. They looked pleased they'd been sold and, in view of the conversation, forever grateful they weren't being kept around the holding pens to possibly be sold off by the pound for the rendering plants. They loved their new master for that alone and each knew they'd do everything possible to keep him happy, no matter what he asked of them.

Late that afternoon and throughout the night, the doctor methodically tested the anal and oral skills of each of the five new stocks. When he was through using their bodies, he ordered each of them to fuck his Hispanic, his Italian and his black and then to have those they'd fucked suck each of them off to test for multiple output capabilities. By midnight, he finally drifted off to sleep, satisfied he had made the purchase of a lifetime. They were all extremely well trained, eager to please him in every way, and seemingly indefatigable, shooting off just as vigorously the second time around as the first. The doctor knew he could sell them for thrice what he paid for them any day of the week. Yes, his life was looking up!

———

All went as planned. The consortium delivered exactly as promised, the dealership was purchased with cash, his salary guarantee was put in writing, and all the sales agents delivered stock as promised. Within a month, the new dealership was filled to overflowing and the doctor was kept busy classifying the selective stock they were receiving. The drug companies and surgeons were consuming the new products even faster then they could be obtained and classified, so a waiting list was developing in the sales department. Profits were far greater than originally anticipated in that their main competitor, Goldsmith & Barnes, had made a bad mistake of replacing their chief classifier, the doctor, with a slave vet they had purchased. He made several bad mistakes in classification and the drug companies grew leery of purchasing further stock there. The same mistakes were being made in delivering slaves for body parts - the slave vet let several through with defective organs and the surgeons refused to deal with Goldsmith & Barnes any more. Profits soared and the original yearly estimates were surpassed within five months of operation. The doctor's minimum salary guarantee was a standard joke among the consortium. His 10% holdings of the stock yielded $720,000 after one year of operation and were projected at $1,350,000 for the second year.

Although the doctor never saw his silent partners, let alone socialized with them, he could care less. He moved from his simple apartment, now crowded with his stable of 8 sex slaves, to a mansion built to his specifications right outside town. There, everyone had plenty of room and it offered his 8 sex slaves plenty of work to keep their physiques in top shape in maintaining the grounds and adding improvements from time to time. In time, the Slave Dealers Association gave him their top award for "Efficiency in Slave Sales," an honor he cherished, especially since he still wasn't invited to their semi-annual dinners due to his ex-slave status.

But who cared! He enjoyed his work; he enjoyed his stable of ready and willing slaves almost every minute of his off-time, and he enjoyed the envious looks of all the freemen far less successful than he was in the business world.

He especially enjoyed flaunting his wealth when he took all eight of his sex slaves out for a little walk, or took them shopping, or simply paraded them around the public parks, all eight cleanly shaven, glistening with oil, tit ringed, collared, and genitally banded and generally showing hard as he led them around by leashes attached to their genital rings as the populace avariciously ogled their naked bodies and the slaves tried to hide their deep humiliation and shame at being so wantonly displayed. It was, in a word, an ending he never dreamed possible when he'd first started out in his medical practice, struggling to please his demanding patients and well aware of their appraisal of him as arrogant, rude, and conceited.

Yes, it had all turned out so well!

A Boner Book

CHAPTER 16

AN AFTERNOON IN THE PARK

A MONTH LATER:

It was a beautiful fall day and the doctor decided to take a pleasant stroll through the park located near his estate. As was his custom for such public outings, he took his entire herd of eight pleasure slaves with him, all freshly shaved, totally naked, and led by the leashes attached to their genital rings for maximum show. The slaves were used to such display by this time, but still showed some embarrassment and shame at their wanton display, a phenomenon which their master enjoyed most about these little outings. The doctor knew it wasn't just from their total body exposure, their erect organs, and the leash frequently tugging at their ball sacs. All slaves got used to that soon enough. No, it was from all the fully clothed people staring at them, all the while making their little comments and jokes as they usually did when slaves were so blatantly exhibited, especially slaves who were obviously kept for sexual usage.

"I bet that black one's something to fuck, don't you, Jim?" one teenager commented to another, staring at the doctor's black slave's huge genitals. "I wouldn't mind going up that black hole myself," the teenager said, pointedly rubbing his crotch.

"You'd get lost up there, Stan," his friend replied. "I bet he could take an elephant up his hole and barely notice it as much use as he's probably had, but they say blacks are really good in sucking - something about their tongues being rougher or something. You ever had a black slave stuck you, Stan?"

"Just once, Jim, but I don't remember anything special about it one way or the other. Of course, the black slave that sucked me off didn't look anything like that one over there. He was just some meat I rented in that brothel over on 10th street - dirt cheap - so you don't get anything like the quality leashed by his balls over there."

"How much for that Italian slave?" another stroller asked the doctor. "He's a real looker and I assume you trained him well."

"He's mighty expensive," the doctor laughed. "But let me assure you he is extremely well trained. There's not a thing in this world that boy can't do to pleasure his master or mistress and do it with zest. I imagine at this point he would bring close to one million on the open market."

"God, that is expensive," the stroller responded. "Too rich for the likes of me. But," he said staring at the Italian slave's rampant prick quivering in the fall breezes, "he looks like he's worth every penny of that million dollars. You ever rent him out so the rest of us blokes could at least sample him now and then?" the stroller joked.

"It's a thought," the doctor laughed. "In the interim, save up. Before long, you'll probably have enough to get something like that on the installment plan. You'd be surprised what you can get at the markets nowadays for $25,000 to $35,000 down payment. With a decent income, you could easily make the monthly payments and think how much fun you'd have with something like this to fuck anytime you wanted."

Comments like this were steady as long as the bevy of eight sex slaves were kept in full display and the doctor was having a great time knowing others were envious of his fine possessions. When some of the viewers asked to handle some of the stock, he let them as long as they didn't bring any of the slaves to orgasm. Consequently, each of the eight slaves got routinely handled rather extensively on such outings: balls hefted and weighed, shafts vigorously stroked, pecs and tits massaged and fondled, assholes explored with an endless succession of fingers pumping in and out of them, and even fingers being inserted into their mouths to test the texture of their tongues and sucking abilities. He realized that if he ever needed ready cash, these boys were better than any money in the bank. He could sell them that very afternoon if need be - and make a huge profit on each and every one of them in the process. But the slaveboy's weren't just a great investment. Ownership of such fine slaves gave him a sense of accomplishment and power he truly enjoyed - even more than their cash value.

"Kraus," the doctor ordered the young German slave. "Get over here and position," as he jerked on his genital leash.

"Yes, master," the blonde German boy instantly responded, grimacing from the pain in his ball sac from the sharp tug on his genital ring, as he quickly assumed the commanded display position, thrusting his genitals forward for full exposure.

The doctor reached down and unhooked the leash from his genital band and, commanding the slave to now kneel, refastened the leash to his nose ring, installed less than a month ago. "There now, Kraus," the doctor said as he pulled on the leash until the slaveboy's face was drawn forward, "this will help keep you from thrashing around when you're being fucked."

"Here, master?" the slave responded, his eyes darting around at the many pedestrians walking by ogling the doctor's display of naked slavemeat. "Right here... in... in... Front of everyone, master?" the German boy stuttered, his whole body reddening in embarrassment

"Of course here, Kraus. It's a beautiful day and we should take advantage of the beautiful weather. It will be good for you to be fucked here in the fresh air," the doctor blithely responded. "Besides," he added, "I'm sure all these good people strolling through the park would enjoy seeing a good German slaveboy being thoroughly fucked. I'm surprised you had forgotten so quickly that one of your primary duties is to bring pleasure to others, slaveboy," he added threateningly. "Perhaps you need a good lashing to remind you of your purpose, Kraus."

"I remember, master," the slave said fearfully, blushing again.

"Sucker, get over here," the doctor addressed his mulatto slaveboy as he tugged on his genital leash, "and position yourself in front of Kraus' mouth. I've got a treat for you today, boy. Instead of sucking a prick down your throat, you're going to stuff that big prick of yours down another slave's throat. You think you'd like that, slaveboy?"

"Yes, master," Sucker responded enthusiastically.

"But don't you shoot off, Sucker," the doctor warned, "because just as soon as Kraus here has your prick hard as a rock and throbbing in need, I want you to pull it out and then thrust it up Kraus' ass just as far as you can and then you hump Kraus vigorously until he either shoots off of I tell you to stop. But Sucker, don't you go shooting off yourself. I want you showing hard all afternoon and besides, I may want to use you again later on or loan you out to one of my friends for their pleasure."

"Yes, master," Sucker replied eagerly, his huge shaft already twitching in anticipation of feeding his prick down someone else's throat for a change.

The doctor jerked on Kraus' nose ring. "Open that mouth wide, Kraus. Sucker going to be feeding you his huge prick and I expect you to swallow it down the whole length and get those throat muscles massaging Sucker's shaft. All these people here," he pointed to a growing number of by-standers gathering for the show, "want to see those throat muscles of yours in action when they massage Sucker's prick. I'm going to leash you by the collar now," the doctor said as he snapped the leash loose from the slave's nose ring and snapped it to the collar ring, "in that being leashed by your nose is just going to get in the way of your duties now."

"Yes, master," the German slave said as he opened his mouth wide, blushing bright red in abject humiliation when he noticed all the people staring at him and then, closing his eyes, swallowed the mulatto's huge shaft far down his well-trained throat and began working his throat muscles on the intrusion as he fought the ever familiar gag reflex and struggled for air - two responses he still had never completely overcome despite all his training and forced practice to date.

"He's a good sucker, isn't he Dad?" a young teenager commented to his father as they both witnessed the public sucking of the mulatto slave. "But I don't know if he's any better than Dado, do you?"

"Well, Dado's older and a lot more experienced, son. Besides, they say North Africans are the best natural born suckers in the world. We're just lucky to own a slave like Dado. You you don't run across them too often," the father counseled. "Still, the German slave is doing a pretty good job of it, judging from the expression on that mulatto's face," he laughed. "That brown slaveboy looks like he's in heaven, and, I suppose if you're named Sucker, getting sucked for a change of pace is being in heaven."

"I don't see how slaves can swallow so much meat without gagging, no matter how much they're trained," another park visitor commented to his friend. "But they all seem to be able to, especially if you've got a whip in your hand," he laughed.

"I think you've put your finger on it, Jim. Whip-training is essential to produce a good well-trained mouth, they say," his friend replied.

Kraus, hearing all these remarks, turned crimson in shame and a few tears begin to spill out of his eyes, but he continued his vigorous throat massage of the mulatto's shaft with no let-up.

"OK, Sucker," the doctor ordered with a little tug on the slave's leash. "It's time to start some serious fucking. You, Kraus, on your hands and knees with your knees wide apart and your ass spread wide and up high for a thorough reaming."

"Yes, master," both slaves said in unison as first Sucker extracted his shaft from deep down Kraus' throat and Kraus bent forward and spread his legs as commanded, lifting his ass slightly to best present his hole.

The doctor reattached the leash to Kraus' nose ring and jerked his head forward. "Everyone will want to see your face when Sucker rams it to you," the doctor commended as he pulled Kraus' face forward as far as it would go considering he was on his hands and knees. "I especially enjoy seeing your neck muscles straining and the sweat pouring off of you when you're taking a big one up you."

"Yes, master," Kraus replied as he felt his nose ring painfully pulled forward until his face was parallel to the ground and totally exposed in perfect profile.

"Go to it, Sucker. Ram it right up there and fuck the shit right out of this good-looking hunk of slaveflesh," the doctor ordered to the applause of the small crowd enjoying this afternoon sport.

"Yes sir, master, sir," Ram said as he quickly mounted the German's slave's body and did exactly as he had been told without hesitation, ramming his shaft all the way up the slave beneath him in one mammoth shove.

"Oh...oh...agh...," Kraus groaned as his body felt like it was being split in two. Every muscle in his body contracted and sweat broke out in every pore as the pain seemed everywhere. His eyes grew wide with fear as his brow furrowed in pain and the large muscles in his 20" neck strained against the confines of his wide tightly fitted metal collar.

"Steady, Kraus," his owner counseled as he tugged on his nose ring to reassert control. "A good solid fucking is always good for a slaveboy - you know that," he reminded his possession, but the German slave was in too much pain to respond just at that moment.

The doctor grabbed his slave whip and wacked it across the rump of the mulatto slave. "Fuck the bastard harder, slaveboy." The whip rained down twice more for emphasis. "Kraus won't break - getting his ass fucked is good for him. Now you fuck that slaveboy's ass deep and hard," he commanded, backing it up with another slash across the mulatto's rump.

Sucker moaned from the whipping, but responded immediately: he plunged in and out of the German slave's asshole as far as he could go with an astounding tempo that left him gasping for breath within a few minutes.

"This hard enough, master?" Sucker gasped as he continued the fierce pistoning.

"Keep it up, Sucker," the doctor responded. "We want Kraus to know he's been well fucked, especially since he enjoys it so much here in the fresh air in front of everyone."

"You still don't like it when you get fucked by a man, do you, Kraus? I can see the resentment all over your face."

"No, master, I don't like it, master. But, master, here in public in front of everyone.... it's even worse," he gasped as the tears flowed down his cheeks and he openly started crying right in front of everyone.

"Pride is unbecoming in a slave, Kraus, and no one feels sorry for you if that's what you're trying to do. A slave's duty is to do what he's told. You should be grateful you're getting thoroughly fucked by a good looking slave like Sucker here - especially here in public where you can please not just your owner but all these other people enjoying this little diversion. You should be thanking us instead of whining around," the doctor said, pausing for the suggested response.

"Thank you, master," Kraus choked out as the tears continued to rain down on his handsome face struggling to accommodate the pain of the intense fucking.

"There, that's more like it, Kraus. Now just relax and enjoy the pleasures of being fucked by Sucker. He won't stop until you're spilled your load, remember, so, unless you get in the spirit of things, we could be here all afternoon," the doctor laughed.

"Yes, master," Kraus said meekly. "I'll try, master."

"You'll do more than try, Kraus, you will shoot off and it better not be too long either," he said threateningly, waving his slavewhip in the air. "We can't expect poor Sucker to fuck you all afternoon until his prick is chafed and bleeding. Perhaps a little touching up will help?"

"No, master, I'll shoot off for you, master," Kraus quickly responded, fear again clouding his eyes.

After several more minutes of intense pounding into his ass, Kraus did adjust to the initial pain of the invasion and settled into the steady deep pistoning into his asschute. His groans turned into sensuous moans as his prostate responded to the stimulation and his prick swelled to full erection and began steadily dripping pre-cum as the onlookers commented freely on his change in response.

"He's still mighty embarrassed from the way he's blushing, Claude, but you can see that stud fucking him is getting a good response. Look at that prick - it's already fully erect and getting ready to pop," an older gentleman commented to his friend.

"Best thing for a slave, Bill, is to fuck them regularly. Reminds them of what they are and avoids all this uppity crap you see in some slaves now and then. Every time I see an uppity slave, I see a slave that needs to be fucked right in front of everyone just like this boy here. Teaches a slave his place in the world, that's for sure, Bill."

"You're dead right on that, Claude," Bill nodded his head in agreement as they both watched the slave under discussion suddenly tense up, groan in ecstasy as his eyes widened and his breathing turned into gasps and then proceeded to shoot a full load in jet after jet from his pulsating prick onto the ground beneath him. The mulatto slave continued to pound into him but was obviously enjoying the squeezing his own shaft was getting as the slave beneath him contracted his ass muscles with each orgasmic outlet.

"OK, Sucker, that's it. Good job, slave. You can pull that monster out now. Kraus has shot his load."

"Yes, master," Sucker said as he jerked his rampant shaft out, quivering in need. Sucker looked pleadingly at his master.

"No, sucker," the doctor said. "We want to keep you hard and ready for some possible use later this afternoon like I told you."

"Yes, master," Sucker said, trying to hide his frustration.

The crowd broke into applause at the completion of the fucking. When the doctor ordered Kraus to lick up his own cum from the sidewalk so as to not leave a mess, they drifted away, knowing it was unlikely any further demonstrations from the gorgeous looking slave stock would probably not be forthcoming. Most stopped to thank the doctor for his generosity in sharing his good looking slave stock with the public on this beautiful autumn afternoon. It was always fun, they noted, to see handsome slave boys put to proper use.

CHAPTER 17

OLD ACQUAINTANCS

"Doctor?" he heard a familiar sounding voice, and turning, saw a vision from his past. "Jim Williams here - from Williams Stud Farm a few miles out of town."

"Mr. Williams," the doctor responded as he recognized the prominent slave breeder who had once offered to buy him in a shopping center and later fucked him at his farm when his former master Adam had taken a couple of black slaves to be sold to him as studs. "It's good to see you again, although," he stared meaningfully at Mr. Williams, "circumstances have certainly changed for me, at least."

"Apparently, doctor. Apparently. Unless slaves can own slaves now, I take it somehow you're not a slave anymore," Mr. Williams commented non-judgmentally. "How'd that happen?"

"Well, I had been enslaved by error and the courts corrected it, manumitting me a few years ago."

"Well, looking at this stock you're displaying today, you've done all right since then," he replied jovially.

"Yes, I have," the doctor replied humbly.

"Well, doctor, I don't know how you felt about being a slave, but I want to tell you first hand you were one good looking hunk of meat and you were great to fuck. I would have bought you in a minute as a stud for my operation if your master would have sold you to me. As it was, he did let me fuck you the day he delivered those two black studs out to me and I'll never forget it - which is really saying something as much as I've fucked slaves over the years."

"I'll take that as a compliment," the doctor replied.

"Damn right you should," Mr. Wilson retorted. "I sure didn't mean to insult you by reminding you of your slave background, but, hell, you were one hot looking slave and fucking you was a real turn-on, let me tell you. No insult intended, of course. When you were a slave, you had to do what you were told of course. Looks to me you're taking advantage of the market with this passel you're parading around today," he added as he visually carefully examined the bodies of each of my leashed slaves.

"While you're ogling my slaves, tell me what happened to those two black studs my master Adam sold you that day," the doctor asked pleasantly. "You still have them?"

""You bet, doctor. They're humping day and night tirelessly and seemingly enjoying it thoroughly. I fuck them myself every now and then and they seem happy in their new life. They're damn productive too. They can sink a sucker in one or two tries every time no matter who they're put to and they still hold up to studding five to six times a day with a full load each time. Some slaveboys are just natural studs and those two blacks are just that - natural studs. They'd be wasted anyplace else."

"If my master had sold me to you, that's what I would have been doing," the doctor chuckled. "Fucking my head off day and night for the profits of Wilson's Stud Farm. You must have thought I was a natural stud too," the doctor laughed.

"I don't know about that, but with a body like yours, it seems a waste to not improve the slave breed with it through some serious studding. As a slave, you don't have any choice in the matter anyway," Mr. Wilson laughed. "You're told to stud - you stud, whether you're a natural or not."

"See any here you might like to take back to your farm?" the doctor teased. "Inspect them all you want - I'm interested in your opinion."

Without hesitation, Mr. Wilson went to each of the leashed slaves and subjected them to a complete bodily examination right in front of all the public bystanders. Each slave had his balls roughly massaged and weighed for fullness, had his penis stroked to full erection; had his tits fondled until they were fully erect, had all his teeth checked, had every major muscle group prodded and stroked, and, finally, ordered to bend over and grab their ankles, felt several fingers sliding up their ass holes as they were tested for ease of entry as well as tightness.

"All eight are damn fine looking stock and obviously are well trained for what they are: pleasure slaves. But, frankly, doctor, only three of them would probably work out studding out at my farm: the olive-skinned boy Spanish boy, the young mulatto, and the red-head. I really don't need the others in my offerings at this time - I've got plenty of full-blacks, blondes, Latinos, Asians and Italians right now - but those three types are in hot demand right now and they look sturdy enough to hold up to the heavy use they'd be put to out at the farm. If you're interested in selling those three, I'd offer you top price, doctor."

"What's top price, Mr. Wilson?" the doctor looked curious, while his slaves shifted around in great apprehension at this turn of events, never having thought of being put to stud around the clock, although they had heard some slaves were bought for that very purpose. Somehow, endlessly fucking anonymous females they would never see again until they were totally dry made their present life as fuckboys for their master seem extremely appealing.

"1.7 Million for the lot of three, provided they test out fully fertile of course," Mr. Wilson replied. "The red-head's not as muscular and hung as I'd like, but maybe with some heavy exercise we could pump up his physique some."

"1.8 mil and they're yours," the doctor laughed. "I'm ready for a little change anyway and with that price I make a decent profit."

The slaves under discussion tried to hide their great anxiety over their master's decision, but risked whimpering nevertheless,

"Please don't sell us, master," until the doctor's whip quickly lashed into their backs, instantly stopping all slave talk on the matter.

"How dare you open your mouths," the doctor flashed at his slaves. "If your owner wants to sell his property, you get sold. It's as simple as that, slaves. Your job is to please your new master if he decides to buy your miserable hides. This man is looking to buy some stock as studs - if he buys you, that's just what you'll do and do it well, do you hear, slaveboy's?"

"Yes, master. Sorry, master," the three slaves replied meekly as they stared at the ground to hide the tears flowing down their cheeks.

"Well, OK, doctor. I've give you the 1.8 million. If you trust me, I just take them now and send a certified check and the sales receipts over properly signed and notarized tomorrow morning. I'll need your business address though, doctor."

"I trust you, Mr. Wilson, but not to the tune of 1.8 million. Besides, I'd like to have a farewell session with my property. How about meeting you at Goldsmith & Barnes tomorrow at 10 A.M. at their administrative offices. They can notify the transfer of ownership and make sure all the papers are in order as well as handle the banking matters. Surely you can go one more night without having these boys bucking their hips back and forth for the profit of Wilson's Breeding Farm."

"Oh, good enough. Nine AM tomorrow for the official change of ownership. But, doctor, don't drain those boys completely dry tonight," he giggled, "because by noon tomorrow I'll hope to have these boys draining their balls on a regular basis out at my farm. You think they'll take to fucking without any problems - you know, after being fucked all the time themselves? You don't suppose they've forgotten how to do it, do you?" Mr. Wilson joked.

"I imagine the whip will prove to be most instructive in that area of instruction," the doctor shot back. "You never seemed to worry that I couldn't make it as a stud even as you were fucking the stuffing out of me."

"Well, now that you've brought up the topic, there's no chance of bedding you down is there, doctor?" Mr. Wilson inquired with a glint in his eye. "I don't mean as a bed buck or a pleasure slave - I mean as two free men getting it on who are attracted to each other and are bored with all these available slaveboys?"

"Mr. Wilson, as I recall I had trouble walking for at least a full day after you last bedded me down. I don't think I want to go through that again," he laughed.

"Ah, I'll be gentle this time," Mr. Wilson chuckled. "You'll like getting fucked by me when you don't have to open your asshole just because you're a slave."

"I doubt it," the doctor laughed. "But I'll give it some thought. If I ever feel I can take on the challenge, I'll give you a call. Meanwhile, I'll see you at 10 in the morning with the three new studs."

"Oh, doctor," Mr. Wilson interjected. "What's your name? I apologize for using your slave name, but it's the only one I ever knew. I don't think a slave name is going to work on that great big check I need to make out tonight to pay for those three slaveboy's," he jested.

"Dr. Ryan Smith, M.D." the doctor answered. "R - Y- A - N S - M - I - T - H."

"Oh, so you really were a doctor!" Mr. Wilson exclaimed. "Where you a doctor when you were enslaved or have you picked up the credentials since then," he inquired.

"No, Adam labeled me 'Doctor' because I was his personal physician before I was enslaved and sold to him. That's why he bought me - he hated my arrogant condescending attitude when I was his doctor and wanted to make sure being a slave cured me of that."

"Did it work?" Mr. Wilson asked.

"Did what work?" the doctor shot back.

"Did being Adam's slave change your attitude?" Mr. Wilson responded.

"Sure did as far as I can judge," the doctor said, smiling.

"You sure weren't arrogant or condescending when Adam loaned you to me that afternoon," Mr. Wilson confirmed. "Just the opposite as I recall. Very cooperative."

"It was that or the whip, Mr. Wilson, as you well know. But I'm interested, what about now? Have I once again become an arrogant son-of-a bitch now that I'm no longer a slave?" the doctor asked with genuine curiosity.

"Not that I notice, doctor," Mr. Wilson said smilingly. "But you could should afford to be arrogant when they just talked me into parting with 1.7 million dollars," he laughed. "No wonder you seem to be so damn rich for an ex-slave, doctor or not."

The three slaves who'd just been sold soberly reflected on this turn of events and pondered how their lives would change. One thing was the same: they had been sold to be used for sex. Although they'd been fucked repeatedly up to now, they had also been ordered to fuck occasionally. As a stud slave, they knew they'd still be fucked occasionally themselves - it was just that now they would be fucking a lot more than being fucked or sucking someone off. The difference didn't seem that much and was certainly tolerable - especially when they realized that as slaves they didn't have any say in the matter anyway. When they thought of being sold off as work slaves, they realized how lucky they were to get a chance like this and thanked their lucky stars once again for being born with bodies attractive on the open marketplace.

The next morning, the doctor stuffed the three slaves to be sold in the rear compartment of his Mercedes ML450 SUV and headed for Goldsmith & Barnes. The Mulatto, the Spaniard, and the red-head had been freshly cleaned inside and out, body shaved, and polished with a light coating of oil. Despite all this, all three looked a little worn out from last night's heavy usage - all three had been fucked repeatedly by both their master and, under his direction, some of the other slaves. In addition, they had repeatedly sucked off the remaining five sex slaves, again under their owner's overt directions, as a farewell gift. All walked a little gingerly due to their sore assholes and most still felt a little queasy from the quarts of cum they had swallowed last night. Today, the doctor had leashed them by their tit-rings and now their swollen prominent nipples, chewed and sucked on during the night, were getting sore from the constant tugging on their way to the administrative offices.

"Hey, doctor, over here!" a voice rang out. The doctor turned to the salutation and confronted, for the first time since his manumission, his former owner Adam.

""Master," the doctor said automatically before realizing what he was doing and then, blushing, quickly changed it to "Adam." Without realizing it, he had almost sunk to his knees in obedience, but caught himself just in time. "Adam, how goes it?" he replied, trying to sound nonchalant as his eyes swept over his former owner and his slave in tow, leashed by his neck collar. "I see you still have Cofkuby," he commented reaching forward and, with a nod of permission from Adam, squeezing the slave's large throbbing shaft.

"Doctor," Cofkuby purred, obviously happy to see his former slavemate and relishing feeling the familiar hand on his organ.

"Well, doctor," Adam said excitedly, "looks like you're doing quite well from the looks of you and your stock. You certainly look healthy enough - what little I can see of you now with all those clothes covering that beautiful body of yours - and these slaves of yours are exquisite. Quite pricey, I imagine," he ventured.

"I'm selling these three off in a few moments to Williams Stud Farm for 1.7 million, Adam. You remember the stud farm, don't you. It's where you sold two black half-brothers to Mr. Williams as prime studs and that same afternoon, lent me to Mr. Williams for a thorough fucking," the doctor said without a trace of shame, bitterness, or humiliation. "Just yesterday, he wanted to fuck me again, but, as he noted, circumstances are a little different now."

"Indeed they are, doctor, indeed they are. Although you seemed to prosper as a slave, you seem to be equally prospering now that you're - well, I don't exactly know what to call you - an ex-slave, I suppose," Adam replied, also without embarrassment.

"Free, ex-slave, manumitted - makes no difference to me, Adam. I've got a good income, a fine home, plenty of slaves to do most of the work, and even eight sex slaves to make sure my life doesn't get boring. I've got you to thank for most of that, Adam."

"How's that?" Adam raised his eyebrow.

"Well, you released me to the courts without any fuss once you realized you'd make a profit on me, the judge liked you and consequently helped me get settled into my new status in society, and you, Adam, taught me the value of having some handsome, well-trained sex slaves around for my enjoyment since you took it upon yourself to considerably broaden my sexual repertoire. Thanks to the assignment you gave me at the plantation to classify your labor slaves for the rendering plants, drug experimentation, or body organ donors, I've got a great job now doing much the same thing but directly for the drug companies and the surgeons. I have a great sex life and enjoy owning and using slaves just as much as you seemed to when you owned me. You taught me a lot, Adam, whether you intended to or not - but I'm grateful, truly grateful, and really owe you a lot. You taught me what life is all about."

"Well, thanks, Dr. Smith," Adam said, using a non-slave title for the first time in speaking with his former slave. "But you left out the part I thought was most important and, really, the reason I bought you to start with."

"What's that, Adam?" the doctor asked.

"The drastic change in attitude. If I may be candid, doctor, slavery may have been the best thing that ever happened to you. You came into slavery as an arrogant, nasty, disrespectful son-of-a-bitch with a condescending sneer. By the time I took you back to the courts, you had learned how to be a decent human being. That part seems to have stuck judging from our conversation today. Don't take me wrong, doctor, I mean all of this frank talk as a real compliment to you. But I must add, doctor, you were one hell of a sex slave when I owned you - one of the best I've ever had - and, as you know, I've owned a lot of them over the years," he laughed. "I'd buy you again without a moment's hesitation if circumstances ever change again to put you back on the market."

"Who knows what lies ahead of us?" the doctor replied. "Adam, you could be enslaved someday for one reason or another and then I might be the very one to offer top dollar for you. If that ever happens, Adam, you ass will be sore for the first month from all the fucking you'd get and your jaws would be so sore from sucking you'd probably think you'd never get your mouth shut again," the doctor laughed.

"Sounds interesting," Adam smirked. "You realize we could play around some without one or the other of us being enslaved," he added suggestively.

"That does sound interesting, especially if you threw Cofkuby into the deal for a threesome. I do miss having that boy fuck me regularly," the doctor laughed.

"Here's my card. It you're really interested, give me a ring. Cofkuby, as you can see for yourself with his prick dripping like a water faucet, would be most happy to cooperate," Adam smiled. "And, Dr. Smith, thanks for sharing those accolades concerning my period of owning you. I appreciate it and it proves my point - slavery was the best thing that ever happened to you - you're really a nice guy now. Still practicing medicine?"

"Yes, but very specialized, thanks to you," the doctor stated. "Sorting and classifying stock for the drug experiments, sewing up the body parts donors for slaves who survive that program, and culling worn-out stock for sale to the rendering plants. It's interesting and it utilizes my training as a licensed physician. You may not realize it, but the judge had all my certification as a physician reinstated along with my manumission. It's work I enjoy and I'm good at it."

"Yes, I know, from when you were doing the same thing for me as my slave out at the plantation," Adam said.

"Hey, Dr. Smith," Mr. Wilson yelled from a few feet away. "And Adam, good to see you again - you got any more good looking well hung studs to sell me?" Mr. Wilson had three slaves following him, all leashed by their genitals.

"Not today, Mr. Wilson. And, besides, the doctor tells me these three handsome slaves he's got leashed are going to be humping away on your studding benches before the day is out. From the looks of their equipment, they're certainly equipped for the job," he laughed as he reached over to the Spaniard standing nearest to him and hefted the slave's huge ball sac.

"You bringing some slaves to market?" the doctor asked, looking the naked slaves over rather thoroughly that were now standing behind Mr. Wilson with their heads bowed.

"Yeah, needed the cage space for the three new ones I'm getting from you, doctor. These slaves here have been studding for six years now and their sperm output is beginning to go. I'm afraid their studding days are over - it's time for a change. I'm going to try to sell them to some women looking for a good bed buck who can still get it up any time they'd want and who knows how to hump till they drop. That would bring top dollar for them. But if that market isn't here today, I'll sell them to a male who primarily wants a slaveboy to fuck him whenever he wants and just as he wants it. That's worth plenty to a lot of men, you know. Of course, if that doesn't work, I'll just sell them off to a brothel. They always pay pretty well because they can extract the last ounce of energy out of these boys' bodies."

"The three slaves under discussion realized age was catching up with them and were actually relieved that they wouldn't have to stud around the clock anymore. During the past two years, the whip had had to be used on them more and more to insure they readily took on every assigned brood and their scarred backs proved it. If they were sold to a single mistress or master, it was likely the demands on their bodies would be considerably less and perhaps they wouldn't have to be beaten as often to please their new owners. If they were sold to a brothel, they knew they would be worn out fast from the constant work load. All of them had seen many a former brothel slave, once handsome and attractive, sold off to the plantations, mines, and construction companies - their beaten bodies and whip scarred backs still capable of unskilled manual work but little else at that point.

"Well, here's my three slaveboys with the title of ownership already filled out for transfer to you, Mr. Wilson. All we need is a notary public and your check," the doctor said.

"And here's the check, doctor," Mr. Wilson said as the two men, leading the six slaves by their leashes, headed for the notary public's stand.

Within minutes, the transaction was done, and Mr. Wilson was now towing six slaves behind him as he headed for the main auction tent where he planned to sell off his worn-out studs.

"Oh, Mr. Wilson," the doctor said. "I was thinking about your offer to get together sometime. Here's my card. Give me a call and maybe we can work out something. I decided it might be fun to be fucked by someone who fucked me when I was a slave out on loan. I want to see if your technique is any different, as you claimed it would be, just because I'm free status now."

"I'll call you alright, doctor, if you're body's even half as attractive as I remember it. And, yes, I'm generally more gentle and loving when the body under me isn't a slave," he smiled. "You'll like it - I guarantee it."

"Don't leave me out of that scenario, doctor," Adam added. "As your ex-owner and primary user for a decent period of time, I'd sure like to come back and sample the goods now that they're not enslaved. And, doctor, I'll throw in Cofkuby to seal the deal."

"You're both on," the doctor laughed. "We'll have a threesome with Cofkuby some Sunday afternoon. Should be fun. If it isn't, I've still got five good looking sex slaves to make it interesting," the doctor laughed again.

Revisiting his past was fun, the doctor decided, and, surprisingly, wasn't threatening to him in any way. Adam was right. He had changed from an arrogant, up-tight conceited son-of-a-bitch to a relaxed, halfway decent human being who could enjoy what life had to offer. He wasn't bitter or resentful - just the contrary. And to think none of this would have ever happened if it hadn't been a slave for a good period of time. He was eternally grateful! Slavery was indeed a wonderful institution.

ABOUT THE AUTHOR

Bill Smith is a prolific author of well-regarded, well written, and widely read tales of homoerotic male slavery. Previous publications you may enjoy include: *BATES TRAINING CENTER, GUILIANO IMPORTS, THE FIRM, THE BRAZILIAN,* and *THE MARKETPLACE.*

www.ingramcontent.com/pod-product-compliance
Lightning Source LLC
Chambersburg PA
CBHW050658290626
47170CB00015B/1677